*For Vera and Jorma and
to Stewart Richardson and Carl Van Vechten,
heartfelt thanks*

Foreword

~~~~~~

It is the fate of some writers—and never other than excellent ones—to be discovered, petted, encouraged, praised, and then left to their own devices, with everyone assuming that the bright new star has established itself permanently in the literary firmament. Whereupon fashions change, the public attention span lessens, sales dip, publishers clean house, and the previous pride finds itself out of print, invisible, and, with any luck, fair game for rediscovery.

All of us—we who write as seriously as we can—find ourselves, from time to appalling time, out of print. It is a dreadful experience, not unlike sudden impotence, and surviving it may be the fire that proves or disproves us.

When James Purdy began publishing, in the 1950s, it was clear to anyone who would trouble to consider the matter that he was an enormously gifted writer. Indeed, he received public praise of a fulsomeness—the extravagance of enthusiasm—that may have sown envy and maggoty urgings toward revenge in the hearts of many.

I recall my own experience of Purdy's early work, and find

it much like my first encounter with the writings of Updike and Welty (and, more recently, Ann Beattie). I knew I was in the presence of not just another talent, for there are many talents, but a very special one. Some writers move us by their gut, others by their mind, and we wish that the one-half of the gift were more a part of the other. Occasionally—and this is what makes the difference—we come upon a writer who can bring it all together, who can fill us not only with the intended enjoyments of the double job properly done, but with a pride of being a member of a profession that can work such wonders.

Purdy did this to me, and I assumed (do we never learn?) that a career so deservedly well launched would self-propel. That this volume, reissuing Purdy's early work, should be necessary is a disgrace; that it exists is a joy.

The things which appeal to me most about Purdy's work—which make me most grateful—are four: its wit, its eroticism, its quirky, pungent prose, and its compassion.

Most of the important twentieth-century writers are deeply, sadly funny—Joyce, Stein, Proust, Beckett, Nabokov, Borges—and the quiet smile, the head-shaking chuckle, the occasional outright guffaw that Purdy's sly wit permits are deeply satisfying.

The truly erotic is less frequently come by in literature. It is a tactile quality; one smells musk, is aware of breath, is brushed by the skin of the described. It is an upsetting and exhilarating sensation as Purdy has it.

As a stylist Purdy is most curious. His prose, his vocabulary, his punctuation are highly individual, seeming to exist in a realm of their own. Now and again one stumbles over a phrase, an odd choice of word, only to understand, finally, that the proper way often seems the willful or arbitrary at first glance. Purdy is a truly original storyteller, and, as such, he tells his story very much in his own way.

The love Purdy feels for all his people—the most foolish, the doomed, the mendacious, the hopeless, the failed—is a compassion one brings to writing. It cannot be applied, like style or a subject, and it may be what separates the men from the boys.

Purdy is enough of a realist—if we are to judge from his

fantasy—not to be taken in by his latest "rediscovery." Perhaps this book will go out of print one day; I hope it does not, but hold on to your copy: it contains work as hard as a diamond and soft as a heart.

Edward Albee

April 1980
New York City

MALCOLM

Contents

~~~~~~

The boy on the bench

In front of one of the most palatial hotels in the world, a very young man was accustomed to sit on a bench which, when the light fell in a certain way, shone like gold.

The young man, who could not have been more than fifteen, seemed to belong nowhere and to nobody, and even his persistent waiting on the bench achieved evidently no purpose, for he seldom spoke to anybody, and there was something about his elegant and untouched appearance that discouraged even those who were moved by his solitariness. For one thing, he looked like a foreigner who would not be apt to speak English, and his *waiting* look itself was so pronounced that nobody felt like interrupting. He was obviously expecting somebody.

Mr. Cox, who was the most famous astrologer of his period, and also the greatest walker (it is said that he often covered forty miles in one day in fine weather), often passed the palatial hotel, and from his first sight of the young man seated on the gold bench felt a kind of exasperation, interest, and surprise all at once. For one thing, the boy's appearance, he felt, was an *augury,* and this was attested to further by the fact that his sitting

there day after day on the bench could offer no earthly or
practical purpose. Mr. Cox, furthermore, felt particularly responsible for this part of the city—in a spiritual sense, that is.
He had lived here for his entire fifty-odd years (though in
appearance he could easily have passed for seventy or even
eighty), and he felt obscurely that the young man on the bench
offered a comment, even a threat, certainly a criticism of his
own career and thought—not to say existence.

For one thing, nobody had ever sat on this particular
bench that persistently before, and, in addition, no one had
really ever sat on it at all before. A display piece, it had
been placed there as a useless ornament, and even very old
ladies waiting for cabs invariably spurned it, recognizing it
by means of their worldliness and senility for the ornament
it was. But the boy had taken it, had sat on it, had become
part of it. Not recognizing his position with respect to the
bench, it was therefore not surprising that he scarcely *saw*
Mr. Cox, far from greeting that elder gentleman as the latter appeared each morning after his night's study of the stars
and his "charts." Instead, the boy looked at Mr. Cox with
empty and almost blind detachment.

Mr. Cox stared angrily, and the boy stared back, open-eyed
and unimpressed. As Mr. Cox was at that period, in a sense,
the city, the hotel, and, in his own mind, civilization, this stare
on the part of so young a person could scarcely be brooked
much longer. Either Mr. Cox must change the direction of his
morning walks, which would be, if not a defeat, a total revolu-
tion in his way of life, or *he* must recognize the youth on the
bench.

On an extremely fine morning in June, therefore, while on
his way to advise a woman patron, Mr. Cox decided on the
latter course: recognition.

"You seem to be *wedded* to this bench," Mr. Cox said to the
young man.

The boy smiled, and looked at the bench, almost as if Mr.
Cox had addressed it and not him.

"*You,*" Mr. Cox said, fearing perhaps that the boy did not

understand him, either through a defect of the brain, or through ignorance of the language.

"Oh, I'm here all the time," the boy began. "My name is Malcolm."

"Good morning, then," Mr. Cox said, still a bit edgy. "My name is Cox."

Malcolm smiled again, but did not say any more. Mr. Cox, depressed perhaps by such an unpromising beginning, was about to move on again, but something about the boy's openness, benign acceptance of everything, and puzzling *expectancy* made him linger.

"I suppose, of course, you are waiting for somebody. Your sister, perhaps," Mr. Cox began again.

"No," Malcolm replied, his attention meanwhile having wandered far afield, as Mr. Cox could plainly see.

Mr. Cox waited.

"I'm waiting for nobody at all," Malcolm explained.

"But you have such a *waiting* look!" Mr. Cox's exasperation got the better of him. "You've been waiting here—forever! For months and months!"

"You've seen me?" Malcolm was surprised.

"Of course I've seen you. I belong here, you know. This city —this—" and with so much explanation ready at hand for him to impart, he could only at last motion toward the strip of land which faced the sea.

Malcolm nodded. "In a way I suppose I am waiting," he said, a deep but dull look now on his face.

Mr. Cox wore an expression of helpfulness, and somewhat smug understanding.

"Yes?" the astrologer prompted, when Malcolm said no more.

"My father has disappeared," Malcolm said suddenly.

"Well, don't tell me you've been waiting for *him* all this time," Mr. Cox said, for the subjects of tragedy and death were most unwelcome to him, and he took it for granted that Malcolm's father was dead.

Malcolm was thinking over Mr. Cox's question. "Yes," he

said at last, "perhaps I may be waiting for him." And he laughed an agreeable strong laugh.

"Waiting for your father!" Mr. Cox expressed impatience and even derision, which, together with helpfulness and smugness, were characteristic of him.

"I'm afraid I have nothing better to do," Malcolm said.

"Ridiculous!" Mr. Cox was quite put out now. "You see, I took special notice of you," he went on, by way of general explanation, "because nobody has ever sat on this bench before. I don't think anybody should sit on it!"

"Poppycock," Malcolm said with a firmness which rather surprised Mr. Cox.

"I am speaking of the hotel regulations, you know."

"Well, I am a guest here, and I sit where I please." Malcolm ended this part of the discussion.

Rebuffed by this, Mr. Cox was again about to move on, and even forget that he had ever entered into a conversation with the boy, when Malcolm said: "Don't tell me you are on your way."

"I've a great deal on my mind," Mr. Cox said lamely.

"Could you tell me what that might be?" Malcolm said at once.

"I see, of course, that you have not heard of me." Mr. Cox cleared his throat and looked down at his unpolished walking shoes. "I am an astrologer." Mr. Cox now looked Malcolm full in the face.

"People still study the . . . *stars*!" Malcolm welcomed this idea with surprise.

"People!" Mr. Cox drew back in anger. He was about to reply to Malcolm's astonishment when his eye fell on the boy's clothes, which were, it was not difficult to see, of the most expensive stuff—too expensive for the depleted epoch they were in, and of a taste whose exact character eluded him.

"Did I hear you say, then, you had no one?" Mr. Cox began his inquiry again.

"No one?" Malcolm thought for a moment, and then, shaking off this question, continued, as it were, with his own line of conversation: "I would invite you to sit down, sir, but I don't think you want to, and I would not want to ask you if you didn't want to comply."

"Your way of refusing to give information?" Mr. Cox inquired in a bored tone.

"I can give you all the information I have," Malcolm said. "I am, then," he began, "as they say, an orphan, and I have had more than enough to live on, but I have, right now, nothing at all to do. And things are, well, a bit too much for me, you see. So I sit here all the time, I suppose."

"Suppose?" Mr. Cox commented. "You *know*!"

"Well, sir." Malcolm nodded. "Yes, I know."

Mr. Cox was suddenly alone with his thoughts—had he left Malcolm he could not have been more so. He could go on asking questions of the boy, of course, but asking questions was not precisely his forte: it was giving answers which was his life work. At the same time, he did not feel he could leave, with so many things still up in the air. And he was sure, too, that Malcolm did not want him to leave, at least not until they had really *begun*.

Almost reading Mr. Cox's thought, Malcolm said: "I suppose if somebody would tell me what to do, I would do it."

"Would that be wise, though, for one so young?" Mr. Cox asked Malcolm to consider this.

"If I could leave the bench," Malcolm said, and he touched it now with his hands, "I would risk it!

"But my training, you see, sir," he continued, "is very limited—almost to my study of French. My father, you know, knew French very well, and continuously read Verlaine."

"Continuously . . . *Verlaine*?" Mr. Cox asked.

But the boy had gone ahead: "I don't have a head for languages, though, and I'm afraid I have gotten almost nowhere in any other line."

"Then it's a good thing you have plenty of money." Mr. Cox gazed from the bench to the hotel.

"But that's what I'm beginning . . . not to have!" Malcolm cried. "You see, it's running out."

"Then we'll have to hit on something at once," Mr. Cox said, relieved perhaps now that he had got somewhere, at least. Nodding perfunctorily, he took out a small notebook from his breast pocket, on which were stamped the signs of the Zodiac, and said: "When were you born, Malcolm?"

Malcolm was silent.

"Don't tell me you don't know," Mr. Cox scolded.

"I'm afraid you're right: I don't," he admitted.

"Then I don't see how you expect me to help you." Mr. Cox was very much put out, and he closed his small notebook with a bang. "I don't think I ever met anybody who didn't know when he was born!"

"But since *he* disappeared, I've had nobody to remind me of dates." Malcolm appealed to the older man.

"You mean to tell me your father never talked with you about plans?" Mr. Cox hammered away now. "Plans for when you were grown up?"

"Grown up?" Malcolm hesitated on that phrase, for it was the first time he had ever thought it would be applied to him.

"Grown up," Mr. Cox repeated, severely gloomy.

"No." Malcolm slowly shook his head, and a faint shadow, perhaps of age, crossed his face for just a moment. "My father," he began—and there was something in the way he said this word which hinted more at ignorance than at knowledge—"my father seemed to feel I was always going to stay just the way I was, and that he and I would always be doing just about what we were doing *then.* That is, sir, going to the fine restaurants, horseback riding and sailing, and sitting in big hotel rooms with him looking at me so proud and happy. He was glad I was just the way I was, and I was glad he was just the way he was. We were both satisfied. You have no idea, Mr. Cox, sir."

"I may have no idea, but I am somehow not surprised."

"We were very happy together, my father and I," and Malcolm sighed faintly.

"Well, I believe that part of your story, but for God's sake, Malcolm, you're not happy now, and you've got to do something about it!"

"Do?" Malcolm exclaimed, and he half got up from the bench.

"Yes, *do,*" Mr. Cox hammered again.

"But what is there to do?" Malcolm appealed to him now. Mr. Cox folded his thin arms over his chest.

"There's only one thing for you to do now," the astrologer exclaimed. "Give yourself up to things!"

"Give myself up to . . . things?" and he got clear up this time from the bench and one could see that Malcolm was neither tall nor short for his age, but looked as if he had always been this height and would continue to be.

Mr. Cox was also rather surprised to see how strong Malcolm looked physically in comparison with the somewhat weaker development of his mental powers.

"Please be seated at once," Mr. Cox commanded.

Malcolm sat down.

"The whole crux of the matter," Mr. Cox continued, "is your father gave you all he had, including his undying affection, I gather, and what have you done with such *largesse?*"

"*Largesse?*" Malcolm wondered.

"I thought you knew French," Mr. Cox assailed him. "*Largesse* is the horn of plenty: it's *everything.*"

"Perhaps if I came home with you, sir—" Malcolm suggested, beginning to feel now how really bad off he was and, probably, had always been.

"Out of the question!" Mr. Cox was firm. "I can only see you, so to speak, on the bench."

"So that we will be passing acquaintances?" Malcolm wondered, briefly.

"I can give you people, though, if it's people you think you are looking for." Mr. Cox softened his refusal. "But I'd rather begin with . . . well, *addresses,*" he said.

"Addresses, sir?"

Mr. Cox nodded.

"That is," the astrologer added, "if you want to give yourself to things—to life, as an older era said . . ."

"I've got no choice," Malcolm cried. "But *addresses?*"

"Addresses," Mr. Cox repeated.

"Here is the first," and the astrologer handed Malcolm what was a calling card. "I want you to take this card." Mr. Cox used his lecturing voice now, although this tone only succeeded in plunging Malcolm more and more into dullness and inattention. "And you are to call on the person whose name is written on it, *today,* at five o'clock."

"I will do no such thing," Malcolm replied, after a long pause, folding his arms, but then suddenly he put out one hand and took the card, and studied it for a moment.

"Why this . . . this . . . is an . . . undertaker's card!" Malcolm drew back in consternation.

"What has his profession got to do with your meeting him," Mr. Cox exclaimed. "You wanted to begin, I thought you said. And Estel Blanc"—the astrologer now named the person on the card—"is after all not going to embalm you!"

"Estel Blanc indeed!" Malcolm's displeasure was intense. Suddenly he threw the card on the ground. "I will have nothing at all to do with such an absurd introduction. And you, Mr. Cox, sir, must have taken leave of your senses."

"Pick that card up at once," Mr. Cox commanded icily. "What on earth would your father think of you if he saw you acting in this manner. You are going to leave the bench and you are going to call on Estel Blanc. Or you can sit here till Doomsday!"

"Addresses," the boy scoffed. "Estel Blanc."

"If you do not obey me," Mr. Cox warned, "there is no reason for our ever meeting again. You were a wealthy boy, I say *were,* mind you, and you have no character and no friends. Sitting here all day long moping over your father, who probably died a long time ago—"

"*Disappeared,* sir," Malcolm interrupted.

"Yet," Mr. Cox continued, ignoring Malcolm's interpolation, "when help in the shape of an address arrives, you wish to do nothing. You wish to remain on the bench. You prefer that to *beginning . . .*"

Malcolm considered this.

"Very well, then." The boy acknowledged his hastiness, and he picked up the card which he had thrown on the flagstone. "I will do as you say in this one case, and because my money is beginning to go"—speaking this last phrase to himself.

"You will do as you are told since you don't know what to do at all," Mr. Cox told him. "And remember the exact hour with Estel Blanc," Mr. Cox warned. "I will call him, and he will be expecting you."

Having covered so much in so short a time, both Mr. Cox and Malcolm felt that they had known one another a great while, and their goodbyes were therefore perfunctory, as in the case of friends of long standing.

"I will see you tomorrow, then, on the bench," Mr. Cox said in parting. "We will discuss your meeting with Estel at that time."

"Understood, sir," Malcolm replied, nodding twice to the elder man, who hastened off now in the direction of the shoreline.

Malcolm looked at the card.

Estel Blanc

Estel Blanc lived in an unremodeled Victorian house with over-size shutters, twenty-five-foot ceilings, and marble-topped ta-bles everywhere. He wore a somewhat long puce jacket with real diamond buttons, so that Malcolm was very much at home at once, for he thought that he and his father were traveling again, and that they had met Estel in their travels.

Furthermore, Estel had had the thoughtfulness to prepare some Spanish chocolate for them to refresh themselves with.

They sat there at five o'clock, therefore, spooning out the chocolate and eating toast along with it, when Malcolm's eyes fell on some unusual paintings which were hanging loosely on all the white walls of the room.

"Did you paint these, sir?" Malcolm wondered.

"No, no." Estel put down his chocolate cup. "*I* paint? I hire them done."

"They are quite out of the way," Malcolm told him.

"Thank you," Estel said. "They were out of the way, it is true, once, and although they are out of the period now, they can somehow always be relied upon to fetch compliments. That is why, in the main, I have them: compliment-fetchers."

Estel toyed for just a split second with the highest and largest of his diamond buttons—and then brought out very quickly: "Where did you say you met Mr. Cox?"

Estel Blanc's question was so sudden and so loud and the Spanish chocolate so thick that Malcolm choked and had to be patted, finally, on the back by his host.

"I'm afraid I have been a little impolite." Estel apologized for his question, but Malcolm could only signal to him that he was not yet ready to go on conversing with him, and in the rest between conversations, observing Estel more closely, Malcolm saw, once his eye had been coaxed away from the puce jacket and the diamonds, that Estel Blanc had the darkest skin of any person he had ever seen.

Left to himself in conversation, Estel could only ask questions now to which Malcolm could reply by nodding or shaking his head:

"Could you have met Mr. Cox at the Raphaelsons, by chance?" Estel wondered. "No, don't try to answer! Let me guess."

Malcolm, however, to be helpful shook his head now, meaning he had not met Mr. Cox at the Raphaelsons, and as he did so his coughing became more acute.

"Mineral water?" Estel wondered, and when Malcolm nodded, Estel brought him a tall Venetian glass which he had had all ready, perhaps, for just such a contingency.

"I met Mr. Cox on the bench," Malcolm unexpectedly brought out after he had consumed only a small volume of the water.

"The bench? . . . Of course," Estel said. Then suddenly reflecting that he had said *of course* to something he had not understood in the least, the host cleared his throat, shifted his legs on the chair on which he was seated, and said in a loud, almost menacing, voice:

"*What* bench?"

"The bench . . . he is going to get me off of," Malcolm cried.

"Go on, go on," Estel said, concentrating intensely.

"The bench I sit on in front of my hotel," Malcolm brought out.

Estel Blanc nodded faintly, and touched his nostrils with a heavy handkerchief which he took out of his breast pocket, and his host was too polite, Malcolm decided, to continue this part of the conversation with further questions. Estel was, however, about to say, *You met him, then, by chance,* when Malcolm, trying to assist the conversation along, said:

"You are, I believe, Mr. Blanc, in the profession of undertaking."

Estel lowered his chocolate cup, which he had been about to place to his lips, and said, after a rather patient pause: "Just call me Estel when we are conversing like this *tête à tête.*"

"But as to your question in regard to my profession, that of *mortician*"—Estel Blanc looked deep and thoughtful—"I have retired as of this spring. I'm forty, you know, and I was losing my art—frankly. People hadn't quite begun to notice that my powers were going, but *I* had. And *I* was what was important to my profession: later the world will know that. And, young man"—here he looked at Malcolm with as firm a scrutiny as if he had held a monocle, or even a telescope, to his eyes—"I was proud of my profession, inordinately proud, no matter by what name it was called!"

"I didn't mean to imply, sir, that it wasn't a fine profession."

"Say no more," Estel warned. "We've concluded the topic! More chocolate?"

"No thank you, sir, it was very rich."

Estel had set his mouth to say something which, by his expression, should have been important, when a peremptory rap was heard from behind a large Chinese screen which closed off the furthest section of the room in which they were sitting.

"We're not ready, Cora," Estel shouted to the screen. "Not ready at all!"

"What on earth was that?" Malcolm wondered.

"Cora always wants to begin before I've half talked to people." Estel reminded himself that Malcolm was not the usual kind of guest. "We always offer entertainment to visitors."

Estel made an attempt at explanation, brushing off a few crumbs of the toast which clung to his jacket and buttons. "I have so many entertainers around still from the old funeral-parlor days, you know . . . And I feel I owe them something, frankly."

"You must be extremely . . . well-fixed," Malcolm said, feeling some sort of compliment should be in order.

Estel Blanc smiled restrainedly. "Well, Malcolm, I like to feel, to quote my white friends, *comfortable.* But *rich*—that is another matter," and he tapped Malcolm's knee with one of the unused chocolate spoons.

"I understand," Estel Blanc continued, "from Mr. Cox, that you have lost a very dear father? Am I right?" and at that moment Malcolm thought he could detect for the first time this evening the exact manner and bearing of the *undertaker* in Mr. Blanc's voice and gesture, especially with regard to his eyes and hands.

"Yes," Malcolm replied slowly, "my father's death or disappearance—no one knows which it really is—has left me with very little to fall back upon."

"It is nice, however," Estel said, in a rather nasal tone now, "that speaking of *comfortable,* he left you in such pleasant circumstances, shall we say."

Malcolm shifted in his seat, and was about to reply to this statement when a loud clapping was heard from behind the same screen.

"Excuse me," Estel Blanc said in a cold but dignified tone, "but it seems we *are* about to begin."

Estel walked over to the high mantel over the fireplace, picked up a small box, extracted from it an oblong tiny disk, lit it, put it on a burner, sniffed it, and quickly resumed his seat near Malcolm.

"Cora Naldi always insists on incense for her number," Estel said. "As I think I said, she used to be in my funeral choir, you see."

Malcolm nodded.

Estel Blanc's hand fell to a light switch, which he touched gingerly, and the lights in the room dimmed considerably. A gong sounded from an indeterminate part of the room.

A white hand removed the screen which had separated this section of the room from Malcolm and Estel, and from behind this a pair of heavy curtains was exposed, these then suddenly parted, and the two conversationalists were brought face to face with Cora Naldi.

Malcolm was never able to tell anybody later what or who Cora Naldi was. He was not even sure at times she was a woman, for she had a very deep voice, and he could never tell whether her hair was white, or merely platinum, or whether she was colored like Estel or white like himself. She both sang and danced in loose shawls, and gave a kind of recitatif when her throat got tired from her singing numbers.

One song, which she sang two or three times, went:

> *And is it so that you were there?*
> *And is it so you were?*
> *And is it so that while you were*
> *Cherries were your ware?*
> *Pale cherries were your ware?*

But Malcolm's attention to her was, in any case, continuously disrupted by the fact that Estel Blanc talked to him during the entire performance, explaining how he had written all the music which Cora Naldi was singing.

The strong perfume of the incense, the overrich quality of the Spanish chocolate, and the bombarding of his ears with both Cora Naldi's songs and Estel Blanc's comments made Malcolm, as Estel Blanc later told everybody, not a receptive audience.

Indeed, Malcolm must have dozed off from time to time, for, after a while, he was awakened by Estel Blanc's rich baritone voice talking to him alone—the little Chinese screen was up again, the curtain was in no way in evidence, and with those were gone likewise the smell of incense and the sound and presence of Cora Naldi.

"I am puzzled," Malcolm heard the baritone voice of Estel

Blanc saying, "by your coolness, detachment, and lack of recep-
tivity." And Estel went on to wonder, perhaps to himself, although he spoke out loud, if this coolness on Malcolm's part did
not have something to do with Estel's "racial strain," as he put
it, or indeed to Malcolm's possible prejudice against Estel's
having been in a profession which is seldom looked upon as
aesthetic, though, as he immediately pointed out, undertaking
is perhaps the most aesthetic of all professions, and indeed the
most universal.

"But I am not sure what you mean by receptive!" Malcolm
cried, seizing on this one word out of Estel's discourse. "And
I do like you, Estel, and I am willing to just forget you were
an undertaker or a mortician or a . . . a . . . *Abyssinian,* or
anything!"

"Oh, dear God," Estel implored, and he immediately got up
from the chair he had been conversing in, and began hurriedly
pacing up and down the room, repeating somewhat religious
exclamations of displeasure.

"Overlook anything I may have said, sir," Malcolm begged
him—"especially if it has offended you!"

Estel only shook his head, meaning Malcolm had again said
the wrong thing, and continued his pacing and his religious
exclamations.

Then, perhaps relenting, the older man said, "But, of course,
Malcolm—your age. That is what it all comes to, naturally."

The storm had lifted, and Estel laughed.

Going up to Malcolm, he opened the boy's jaw, looked in at
his teeth; then pushing back his head, he looked carefully at his
eyes.

"You're not more than fourteen!" Estel told him. "Mr. Cox
said you were all of fifteen!"

Pacing again about the parlor, Estel went on: "But what does
it matter, actually: fifteen or fourteen, or twelve. I have, since
childhood, always lived among the mature, and indeed, if I may
say so, the overripe." The dark man laughed with somewhat
histrionic bitterness. "I am afraid I have forgotten there was
youth—in your case, dear Malcolm, almost infancy . . ."

And he suddenly went over to Malcolm and shook the boy's hand.

"Come back in twenty years, and we shall understand one another," Estel said, and he ushered Malcolm rather hurriedly in the direction of the door.

"But I would ever so much like to come back again," Malcolm said. "I . . . enjoyed it all, sir. It was . . . *travel* to me."

"Travel?" Estel Blanc considered this, dubiously. "No, I am afraid I cannot see you again soon, or indeed at all," and he pulled at the sleeves of his jacket.

"I am flattered, of course," Estel went on, "that Mr. Cox should have thought of me as a kind of introduction for you to a greater world. But I am not in my element with the immature. I must be firm about this. I am not in my element . . . But come back, like I say, in twenty years!"

Having entered a slightly greater environment from the one the bench and the hotel had for such a long time given him, Malcolm was somewhat loath to allow the door of Estel Blanc's house to close on him. He stood as long as decency would allow him on the threshold; then, seeing that there was no way to prolong his visit, he stepped out onto the pavement, and in doing so—as he was to tell Mr. Cox the next day—walked right into the open arms of a policeman.

Coming out of the police station two or three hours later, whom should Malcolm see waiting for him but Estel Blanc himself, muffled up in a light coat which he wore in the manner of a cape.

"You said twenty years," Malcolm cried, and the thought actually did cross his mind that perhaps after all he had been imprisoned in the police station for that length of time.

"An auspicious beginning to your career," Estel said, somewhat pleasantly, somewhat acidly, for that was his permanent manner. "I saw the police sergeant make the arrest," the dark man said, "and although our *soirée* together was a total failure, I did feel some small sort of responsibility for you. I'm so relieved they let you off, of course . . ."

"The police captain and the sergeant both were very kind to me," Malcolm reflected, "once they found out I was not the person they were looking for."

Estel nodded, waiting for more.

"They said it was a confidence man they were after, and my good clothes, for a moment, led them to think I was he. But when they saw that I was not . . ."

"When they saw you were not a grown man." Estel bobbed his head up and down. "Yes, everything is permitted to youth!"

"But how did you know?" Malcolm seemed thunderstruck.

"I know the police," Estel remarked.

"The police sergeant, who was the one who had arrested me," Malcolm went on pointedly, "even invited me back."

"Invited you back. That is real success!" Estel told him.

"I don't suppose *you* have changed your mind, by chance, about me," Malcolm ventured.

"No, no," Estel replied, "*I* am not here to invite you back. Really, Malcolm, you are terribly backward mentally. No, my decision rests just where it did when you left . . . We are not meant for one another's company, and until you are more mature, conversation itself, let alone friendship, is impossible."

The boy looked down disconsolately.

"The main reason why I have been waiting outside for you, in such an undignified position for me—is quite a simple one."

Malcolm smiled, his eagerness returning.

"You see"—Estel fingered a piece of cardboard on which some words had been scribbled—"I am usually Number One on Mr. Cox's list of addresses, and so it was quite natural that he should have entrusted Address Number Two with me—to give to you, of course, when the time came . . . But when the time came tonight, well, I forgot is all!"

"Address Number Two!" Malcolm cried.

"Oh, what enthusiasm," Estel commented. "I sometimes almost regret my decision with regard to you when I hear your freshness of tone. But to business . . . As I said, Cox has entrusted me with giving you Address Number Two. Here, take it, it's yours."

"Address Number Two," the boy read, holding the cardboard reverently, and reading what he saw there: "Kermit and Laureen Raphaelson. Why, what beautiful names . . . Are they also . . ." Malcolm hesitated.

"No, they are not Abyssinians, if that's what you mean," Estel said pointedly, placing the ends of his handkerchief, which seemed to have been dipped in some strong liquid, to his nostrils. "You will, I hope, find them to your taste!"

"Please, please, sir, tell me how it was that I have offended you," Malcolm began again, but a violent movement from Estel's cloak-and-coat stopped the boy.

"And you have stood out here . . . in the cold air waiting for me," Malcolm went on, deeply apologetic.

"Yes, the cold June *cold* air," Estel replied, and he took the boy's hands and shook them with ceremonious restraint.

"Now this is goodbye," the dark man told him. "As I say, your career has begun auspiciously. The police sergeant episode alone is proof you have a charmed life. Keep close to your bench and Mr. Cox's addresses, and nothing can go amiss. And remember, dear boy, when you are mature, come back to see me. I will be here."

Estel bowed, and retreated slowly walking backwards directly to his house, which was only a short half-block from the police station. An old sign,

THE BLANC EMPIRE MORTUARY,

now unlighted, looked down upon them.

"I do wish you wouldn't be so final," Malcolm said, but too low for Estel to hear him.

When the undertaker had disappeared into his house, Malcolm felt very lonely and tired. The events of the evening had been much too exciting and stimulating, and had he not just then looked down and seen the new address, he believed he would have burst into tears. Yes, there could be no doubt, he was beginning life, and with his usual silent evening prayer addressed to his father, wherever he might be, dead or alive, lost or found, he hastened back to his hotel suite.

Kermit and Laureen

Malcolm found himself the next evening in a long hall waiting for the buzzer to admit him to the apartment of Kermit and Laureen Raphaelson.

But as the buzzer had not worked for many weeks, perhaps even years, Laureen herself appeared to open the door, a stout young blond woman whose face was covered with white moles.

She wore a look of extreme suspicion, together with mechanical expectation and boredom.

"You're from Professor Cox?" she said.

Malcolm nodded.

"The little man is not in his parlor yet," Laureen said, ushering him into her home.

"He is not?" Malcolm replied, wondering to whom she was referring.

"As a matter of fact," Laureen continued, and they now entered the front room of the apartment, "he is in the pantry finishing his supper. He often eats in there alone now just to spite me. He refused to eat even his cabinet pudding with me tonight. I am afraid Professor Cox may be right, and we are headed for the divorce courts."

Laureen pointed out a large overstuffed chair for Malcolm to sit down in.

"Divorce courts are entirely out of my range of experience," Malcolm told Laureen. "But I am sorry you are headed for them."

"I haven't said a divorce is actually imminent, mind you." Laureen thought better of the subject.

But Malcolm was not listening, for he was experiencing the depth of the overstuffed chair, most of whose stuffing had come off through age onto the floor beneath it.

Malcolm was about to exclaim, "But what a deep chair, Laureen," when the latter cried out: "The little man!" in such a loud voice that Malcolm was startled, and leaped out of the chair, though it cost him great agility and effort to do so.

"You have a caller." Laureen addressed the person who had entered the room.

Malcolm at first mistook the latter for a child, but then realized that, limited though his experience in such matters was, the person was a man, and a midget.

"Why, who are you?" Malcolm could not prevent himself from exclaiming.

"*Her* husband." Kermit Raphaelson, the "little man," pointed with malice and glee in the direction of Laureen.

Malcolm was not only astonished to see that Kermit Raphaelson was a midget but that he looked quite handsome and clever, and differed from any other young man only in the matter of size: one merely felt one was looking at him with the wrong end of the eyepiece.

"I'm so glad to see somebody fresh and young!" Kermit cried. "And don't look so surprised, Malcolm," he continued. "Ignore Laureen, if you like, and pay your best attention to me. *I'm* the lonely one!"

"Good God alive," Laureen cried, raising her eyes to the ceiling. "It's beginning already."

"Yes, we are married," Kermit laughed, sitting down in a small chair specially designed, it was clear, for him. "Married, and married, and *married*."

"I beg of you not to bring on a scene in front of this child."
Laureen turned to her husband.

Kermit ignored her although he shot an oblique black look
from beneath his lowered eyelashes.

"So you"—he turned again to Malcolm—"are the boy who
is infatuated with his father."

"I?" Malcolm pointed a finger at himself. "Infatuated?"

"Professor Cox has already told us all about you," the midget
explained.

"But there's nothing yet to tell." Malcolm protested against
the *all*, which sounded to him both complete and frightening.

"There is a great deal to tell, *always*, Malcolm." Kermit
spoke somewhat gravely now.

"And you really are married," Malcolm said staring closely
at Kermit.

Kermit lowered his eyes. "*She* proposed," he explained,
pointing to Laureen.

"I warn you," Laureen cried. "I will not tolerate your telling
secrets about our marriage to a third party again!" Laureen
continued to stand, perhaps because she had not yet made up
her mind whether to leave or to stay, and because also she was
in an extremely bad humor, which Malcolm's arrival had only
worsened.

"Why did you choose to come to see us, Malcolm?" Kermit
said, edging his tiny chair closer to his guest.

Malcolm remembered his disastrous evening with Estel
Blanc and did not reply immediately.

"Well, why did you come?" Laureen was severe. Both Kermit and she now stared at the boy fixedly.

"*Why* did I come to see you?" Malcolm swallowed, looking
from one to the other, for the contrast between the two was
stupefying to him—Kermit so small, Laureen so large and
plump and commanding.

"Why, Mr. Cox ordered me to," Malcolm admitted under all
the scrutiny and severity.

"You had no interest, then, in us, for ourselves?" Laureen
interrogated.

"None whatever," Malcolm replied without expression or regret or belligerence in his tone.

"We see," Laureen told him, and she smiled quietly triumphant.

"I suppose you know about my evening with Estel Blanc," Malcolm went on.

"Of course we know about it!" Kermit said. "Professor Cox keeps us pretty well informed, you know, as to what all his friends are doing and thinking."

"Professor Cox! That awful old . . ." Laureen began, but instead of finishing what she was to say, she sat down in a tall straight-backed chair, and began rolling herself a cigarette, a process which took a long time owing to her hands trembling so much.

"Professor Cox," Laureen began again when her cigarette was rolled, "Professor Cox has ruined Kermit here with his ideas. We were *so* happy before we met him."

Kermit laughed sardonically at this point.

"Laugh all you wish." Laureen turned her back now on her husband and sat facing Malcolm. "Kermit and I were happy. But that old . . . Malcolm," she said suddenly, "you must give up Professor Cox if you want to grow into a fine and trustworthy man."

"Laureen, my dear," Kermit addressed his wife, "if you are going to sermonize, I will have to ask you to leave the front room, and go out and sit with the cats in the back parlor."

"You should tell Malcolm how many cats you have," Laureen said, "so that he can have a picture of where you are ordering me to go."

Kermit, however, said nothing, but made ironic little faces at Malcolm, who broke out into stifled guffaws.

"We have fifteen cats!" Laureen said in a tragic voice, but then hurrying on, in her telegraphic impulsive style: "Malcolm, am I getting across to you? . . . Professor Cox is not a man whom you should know at your age. I am trying to help you!"

"On what grounds should I not know Mr. Cox?" Malcolm inquired.

"A brilliant rejoinder to her stupid command," Kermit cried.

"Kermit, for pity's sake," Laureen begged her husband. "My husband," she explained, "is scarcely any better than Professor Cox, I am ashamed to admit. But I can see that you, Malcolm, are not yet corrupt . . . Not completely, at any rate." She studied the boy a little more closely.

"Thank you, Laureen," Malcolm told her, and again Kermit exploded into laughter, and Malcolm, receiving this laughter as a compliment, nodded briefly to the midget, and then directed his full attention back to Laureen.

"Professor Cox commands people to be their worst!" Laureen said.

"Nonsense," Kermit interrupted. "He tells them to do what they must do in any case, and they are merely free to be what they have to."

"All of Kermit's metaphysical ideas are taken lock, stock, and barrel from Professor Cox," Laureen said patiently, looking at the bare wood of the floor.

"Professor Cox has a rather low opinion of Laureen at the moment," Kermit informed Malcolm.

"Low?" Laureen said. "Well, not just of me, Kermit," she went on. "He has a low opinion of everybody. Malcolm," Laureen said, moving her chair closer to that of the young boy and as she did so she touched him gently on his empty *boutonnière,* "do you know what Professor Cox suggested only last week to me—this is to show you the danger and the risk you run with him . . ."

Malcolm shook his head.

"But you're so young to hear it!" Laureen reflected. "So terribly young and unaware." She shaded her eyes with her hand, perhaps overcome by the thought of Malcolm's ignorance.

"No one's too young to hear anything about people!" Kermit cried, disgusted. "And where is my hot tea, by the way? I asked you for my tea nearly an hour ago, and all you have been doing all evening is walking up and down complaining over your lot as a woman. If you kept up your womanly duties about the house, brought me my supper on time, and prepared my tea like a decent housewife, you wouldn't have time to be unhappy, wouldn't have time to worry about Professor Cox's commands."

"My dear, didn't I bring you your tea?" Laureen cried. "I won't have it said I have neglected my duties by you, no matter what may happen later on . . ."

Laureen immediately hastened to a small table, where the tea was already prepared, and brought Kermit his cup.

"Will you join Kermit in a cup of tea?" Laureen asked Malcolm, and when the latter nodded, she brought him the same kind of cup which she had given her husband except that this one had a crack in it, which Malcolm stared at some time before finally putting his lips to it to drink.

After sipping his tea with a critical expression for a few moments, Malcolm said in a rather stentorian voice:

"What did Mr. Cox command you, Laureen?"

"My precious," Laureen said, and going up to Malcolm she kissed him on the cheek.

"What a ridiculous display of pretended emotion," Kermit cried, addressing his wife. "I will tell you what Mr. Cox commanded her." He turned immediately to Malcolm.

"Let me tell it, Kermit," Laureen begged him. "I want the boy to hear it without your embellishments."

"Will you allow me to entertain *my* guest in *my* fashion, or shall I ask you again to step into the back room?" Kermit thundered at her.

Laureen bowed her head.

"We are poor people," Kermit began in a trembling voice, while Laureen held her head in her hands, like a woman in a court trial scene. "I make very little as an artist—" and here he pointed in the general direction of the many easels, oil paintings, empty frames, and sculpture which filled the large room. "Laureen, although a brilliant stenographer, can seldom keep a position, owing to her wish to meddle in the higher business of the offices where she is employed. Quiet!" Kermit roared when he saw Laureen make a motion that she wished to speak.

"Knowing my wife's *propensities*," Kermit said vindictively, "Professor Cox merely and sensibly proposed that Laureen go out with certain gentlemen who would pay her for her compliance with their wishes, since she was not entirely unknown for her favors before her sudden proposal of marriage to me."

The midget took out a cowboy handkerchief and wiped his mouth, and examined one of the inexpensive rings on his index finger.

"Laureen had promised me when she proposed marriage to me," the midget continued, "that once I had agreed to be her husband and our visit to city hall was concluded, my days of struggle and difficulty would be over, that I could devote myself solely to my art, and at last achieve the full development and flowering of my talents. The exact opposite has been true. Since the prolonged weekend of our honeymoon in Pittsburgh, there has not been a day or night when we have not worried about food or necessities—I do not mention luxuries—and the little money I had inherited she, incompetent thing, has squandered in her mismanagement! I had to sell my finest oils for a song!"

"Exaggerations, dolly," Laureen cried.

"But, Malcolm"—Kermit suddenly recovered his self-possession—"I did not agree to have you come to our house merely to let you hear about us."

"But it is so interesting and different," Malcolm exclaimed. "You see, there is nothing to hear about in my case. I am, well, as they say, a cypher and a blank."

However, Kermit and Malcolm soon found their attention turned to Laureen, for she was giving what seemed to be a speech:

"When one's husband no longer respects one, when he can tell the most intimate secrets of marriage in front of a third party," Laureen was saying, "there is indeed nothing for one but the *streets*. Malcolm," Laureen said to the young man in particular. "I want you to know what Professor Cox proposed to me."

"What boredom! What repetition!" Kermit said.

"Do I look like a streetwalker?" Laureen demanded, going

directly up to Malcolm. "Answer me, dear boy, for you are not yet corrupt . . ."

When Malcolm did not reply, Laureen drew even closer to him: "Do I, or don't I?"

"But aren't you . . . already one, dear Laureen?" Malcolm cried in consternation. "I thought your husband . . ."

Kermit laughed uproariously, while at the same time he pointed to the back room as a signal for Laureen to leave.

"Go back there and talk to the cats," Kermit ordered her. "I want to have a *quiet* talk with Malcolm. I certainly deserve to see somebody else in the evening beside your own horrible blond self."

"A true pupil of Professor Cox," Laureen exclaimed. Then turning benevolently to Malcolm, Laureen kissed him briefly on the forehead, and with a dramatic gesture of laying her hand across her mouth, she retired into the back room.

After a luxuriant silence, Malcolm asked: "Are there really cats back there?"

"As Laureen said"—Kermit nodded—"there are fifteen."

"How sleepy I am suddenly," Malcolm said.

"Sleepy—at this hour?" Kermit expressed shock.

"Conversation makes me quite sleepy," Malcolm explained. "You see, usually all I have to do with people is have them wait on me. A maid will bring me a cup of chocolate, or the man from the tonsorial parlor will cut my hair and nails, and I exchange a few words with the leader of the string orchestra in the hotel, but no more than that. But since I have met Mr. Cox, I have been having rather long conversations with people, and it has made me quite sleepy."

"Lie down on the sofa and I will talk to you, then, while you rest," Kermit told him.

"I'd rather you didn't talk while I lie down," Malcolm said, and he went over to the sofa and stretched out. "In a little while," he told his host, "you must summon a cab, and I will go to my hotel."

"No, no, you can't leave in such a peremptory manner, not after you just got here, and after Laureen has left so that we can have our private talk!'' Kermit complained.

"But what more is there to talk about? We've covered everything here, haven't we?'' Malcolm cried, lifting his head a little to see Kermit more closely.

Kermit laughed and finished his tea.

"How odd though that Laureen should be a . . . a . . .'' Malcolm mused.

"Odd she's a whore?'' Kermit yawned. "Well, it's the only thing she ever wanted to be, and why she thought marriage would straighten her out, God only knows, especially marriage with me,'' and he picked up one of his paint brushes and inspected it briefly. "I never thought marriage would *straighten* me out,'' Kermit went on. "But I did think it might be a kind of long rest for me. But it's been a real workout, let me tell you, and as I say, never a day passes we don't worry about money.''

The midget sighed and shook his head.

"I do not seem to recognize women like that when I meet them,'' Malcolm remarked.

"You do have beautiful clothes,'' Kermit said, looking at Malcolm.

"Do I?'' Malcolm looked down at himself. "They're all suits my father picked out years in advance of my being this size,'' Malcolm explained. "He has picked out suits for me all the way up to the age of eighteen. I think he had a presentiment he would be called away, and he left me plenty of clothes.''

"Your father *was* quite extraordinary,'' Kermit asserted.

"That's what I tried to tell Mr. Cox,'' Malcolm cried, "but he wouldn't believe me.''

"Oh, he probably believed you,'' Kermit said. "He only wanted to test your belief. To make you talk.''

Malcolm nodded. "But I'm glad *you* think my father was extraordinary,'' the boy said. "You see, he's all I've got. And now I don't have him.'' And a short sob came out from Malcolm's throat.

Kermit looked at his wrists, and then at his empty tea cup.

Malcolm sat up just then, though, laughed, and then immediately lay down again, exclaiming: "I am too sleepy to sit up.''

"I hope you won't command me to stop talking," Kermit said winsomely.

"I would rather you didn't," Malcolm replied, "but if you don't mind me never answering or not really listening, perhaps it's all right if you do go right on talking."

"Very well, then," Kermit said, "I will do just that, because I am awfully fond of talking."

"There is one thing, though, I must get straight before you begin your talking," Malcolm informed Kermit. "Are you a dwarf or a midget?" And Malcolm sat up briefly on the sofa.

"Oh, goodness," Kermit said after a short pause. "I'm neither."

"Neither?" Malcolm was so surprised he sat all the way up and put his feet down on the floor. "Why, you certainly must be one or the other!"

"No, no, *no!*" Kermit said, becoming very red in the face. "How stupid can one be?"

"But you're so small," Malcolm cried. "You *must* be a midget!"

"I'm not big"—Kermit was patient now but sternly emphatic —"but I am no different from other men—fundamentally." He stood on this statement.

"You're just short, then?" Malcolm inquired.

"That's one way of putting it," Kermit agreed.

"But I've seen you in circuses—that is, I've seen short little men like you."

"Not like me!" Kermit shook his head, and he wiped his mustache with his cowboy handkerchief. "You've seen nobody like me," he repeated, and suddenly he stuck his tongue out at Malcolm, and opened his eyes very wide like a movie actor.

"Golly, how awful you look when you do that," Malcolm observed.

"I am awful sometimes." Kermit laughed a bit tunelessly.

"I think I like you, though," Malcolm said. "You're not *usual.*"

"Well, I could say the same thing of you, Malcolm, though I won't," Kermit replied. "You are not too bright, I gather, but you have your own charm, and an air of . . . innocuous fellowship."

"You don't do anything disgusting like embalm people here, do you?" Malcolm wanted to know.

"Oh, back to Estel Blanc again," Kermit scolded. "No, as I told you, I am an oil painter, though nobody ever buys anything that I paint."

"You are the first painter I have ever known," Malcolm informed him. "Of course, I had never known an undertaker either until the other day."

Suddenly they both heard loud outcries in the back room, and soon Laureen rushed out, her hair down, and her dress torn, holding her arm, which had blood on it.

"Peter bit me and scratched me," she cried. She seemed near hysterics.

"Fetch that pitcher over there," Kermit ordered Malcolm.

Malcolm brought the pitcher to Kermit and the latter quickly threw the contents on Laureen.

The water, or whatever it was in the pitcher, was a sooty color and when it had covered her head completely, Malcolm thought that Laureen resembled ever so noticeably Cora Naldi, but of course the two ladies were not at all alike, and Laureen wore no wig, and probably could not sing a note.

Laureen continued to cry even after the water had been thrown on her, but she was less vociferous.

"Now come over here and sit down on the footstool beside me, and I will talk to you," Kermit told his wife.

Laureen obeyed him, and once seated on the stool, she complained softly: "Why can't we get rid of those beasts! They invariably bite and take their spite out on me."

"You must learn to live with them, and love them, dolly," Kermit said, using the same pet name which she had a while before employed for him. He kissed Laureen gently on the hair.

"Live and love, dolly," Kermit told his wife.

They had both almost completely forgotten Malcolm, who was kept standing up waiting to be recognized, and who finally after several minutes walked slowly over to the front door.

"Good night, then," Malcolm cried after several minutes more of waiting, during which the married couple cooed and embraced.

"Oh, Malcolm," Kermit cried. "You're not *going*!"

"I see a cab outside," the boy cried, "and I don't like to be away from my hotel suite much longer, you see."

Kermit expostulated.

"I'll be back, though," Malcolm said. "That is, if you will *let* me."

"But the evening is still young," Kermit explained. Then, resigned to Malcolm's going: "You don't know what marriage is," Kermit called helplessly from his position with Laureen. "But do come again, dear boy. You're awfully different, and it's been more than enjoyable."

"Yes, do come again, dear Malcolm," Laureen cried to him. "And forgive our not getting up. You'll understand when you're married, though."

"Do call us, dear Malcolm," Kermit shouted from beneath the heavy embrace of his wife.

"Thank you for the evening. Thank you for everything," Malcolm cried, going out. "Good night to both of you."

A second visit

~~~~~~

Now that Malcolm was going out into the great world, so to speak, he felt compelled to write down some of the things, at least, which happened to him, for he was sure they were very important, and would be even still more so in the future. But as he had never been to school regularly, owing to his having always been traveling with his father, or waiting for his father to return, he had very little command of language, and could seldom do more than copy down some of the things which his new friends, especially Professor Cox, said.

However, after his meeting with Kermit Raphaelson, Malcolm wrote down a statement original to him, which was found later among his effects: "Married love is the strangest thing of all."

Meanwhile, a small envelope had arrived from Professor Cox, containing Address No. 3, but Malcolm did not open this immediately, but put it in his breast pocket for later study.

The next day, on the bench, Mr. Cox questioned Malcolm concerning his visit to the Raphaelsons.

Pleased that Malcolm had been successful there, Mr. Cox

sighed with relief: "If you hadn't got on with the Raphaelsons, well, I will tell you, dear boy," and he shook his finger at Malcolm, "I would, I am afraid, have had to give you up."

"Entirely?" Malcolm cried.

"Entirely," Mr. Cox said. "I was talking it over with my wife only last night. If he fails again, I said . . ."

"You mean there is a Mrs. Cox!" Malcolm was thunderstruck, for it had never occurred to him that an astrologer would have a wife.

"Of course," Mr. Cox replied. "Everybody is married, Malcolm. Everybody that counts. And you will have to begin thinking about it, too."

"But what would I have done . . . if you had given me up?" Malcolm wondered almost to himself. "I mean, what would I have done about *addresses*!"

Mr. Cox smiled.

"Well," the astrologer mused, "you've got to remember, sir, that you have been off the bench twice . . . And I suppose that in the end—sink or swim, as the old saw has it—you would have *swum*."

"Thank you," Malcolm said.

Then, turning his attention to what puzzled him very much, Malcolm went on: "I don't understand why Kermit will not admit he is a midget."

Mr. Cox whistled shrilly. "He has a certain personal right to deny it, if he wishes to," he said, an air of dubiety about him.

"I asked him if he was one, and he was firm about not being one at all," Malcolm expostulated.

"That is so like Kermit," Mr. Cox agreed. "He has never told anybody that he is a midget. His mother evidently never told him he was one, and never referred to it, so that when finally he grew up—well, he didn't actually know it, his life had been that sheltered. Laureen proposed to him when he was only seventeen, and they were married at once. He has really never known the world, much less, in fact, than you, for at least you have traveled with your father."

"Yes," Malcolm agreed. "I have seen things around me to a greater extent than the little man."

Mr. Cox looked away toward the skyline in the manner of one who has a matter of persistent concern there.

"You're not leaving so soon, sir!" Malcolm exclaimed, for he had a hundred questions to ask of Mr. Cox.

"The day will come," Mr. Cox went on, just as though he had not heard Malcolm's question at all, "the day will come when he will have to admit he is a midget, and go on from there."

"He can't just go on acting like a little man, you mean?" Malcolm put the question to him.

"Not if he is the only one who believes it!" the astrologer answered immediately.

Mr. Cox took out his small notebook with the zodiacal signs on the cover, and wrote down something hurriedly on one of the pages inside.

Then turning his attention briefly to Malcolm, he said:

"Now that you have Kermit to visit, I won't be spending quite so much time with you here on the bench . . ."

"And I cannot visit you, and *your* wife?" Malcolm tested Mr. Cox again.

"Quite out of the question *now*," Mr. Cox said. "Our relationship must remain on a certain *professional* level."

"I see," Malcolm said.

"But I think you are beginning to win *through*," Mr. Cox told him enthusiastically, and shaking hands, he took leave of his young friend.

"Don't forget Address Number Three: they're quite ready for you, you know!" he said in parting.

"I knew you would not fail me," Kermit exclaimed when he saw Malcolm entering the door of his studio. "Come in at once."

The little man dropped his paintbrush, pushed back the easel on which there was a half-completed oil painting, and advanced toward his friend.

"But what's happened to everything?" Malcolm wondered, for nearly everything in the studio had been broken, or thrown about: the plaster casts of gods, masks of celebrities, canvases, articles of furniture—all lay strewn and dismembered as in a junk shop.

Kermit did not say anything for a moment; then as Malcolm continued to gaze wonderingly at him, the little man explained: "Laureen has left me."

"Left *you*?" Malcolm considered this with astonishment.

"Oh, what's so surprising about that," Kermit added, a new kind of bitter quality in his manner. He ushered the boy to a seat.

Kermit sat down now also, on his specially designed chair, but a different one from the fancy carved chair he had sat on at his first meeting with Malcolm.

"What beautiful chairs you always sit in," Malcolm said.

"I make them myself," Kermit explained, without enthusiasm.

Malcolm shook his head in incredulity and admiration.

"Yes," Kermit went on, indifferently, "I have a whole carpentry shop in the back where I make things such as you see around you. It's closed just now. That is, the cats are living out there . . . Before I married Laureen, the cats lived wherever I was, that is, throughout the whole studio, but when she came things had to change. She demanded affection at first of all the cats, and then she was partial to Peter and cruel to the others. Then she tired of Peter and was cruel to him and kind to the others. Finally, she was cruel to all of them. They wearied her. The same treatment was accorded to me."

"I can't get over that you are married at all," Malcolm exclaimed.

A flicker of displeasure crossed Kermit's face.

"I mean"—Malcolm saw the look—"you could have perhaps . . . *waited*."

"I think that is about all one can say about my marriage, perhaps," Kermit said, somewhat enigmatically. "But then who should I have married?" he added as an afterthought, perhaps to himself.

Kermit clapped his hands, and a young man without a shirt on appeared.

"Ginger beer for two people," Kermit commanded.

"Who on earth is that?" Malcolm wondered.

"He is my morning servant," Kermit explained absent-mindedly.

"He has such a powerful build," Malcolm noted.

"He is planning to open a gymnasium in the fall," Kermit explained, "and of course he has to look the part if he is to get pupils. But you do like ginger beer, don't you?" Kermit said, a bit more affable again.

"I don't know that my father and I ever drank ginger beer." Malcolm studied Kermit's question perhaps a bit too pedantically to suit his small host.

Kermit merely said, "Your *father*, I see," and then added quickly: "You have had a long life in hotels, haven't you?"

"Yes, we—that is *I*, now, have always lived in hotels. Big ones and little ones. But now that my father is no longer here, my money is beginning to go, and—" Malcolm said no more, a look of surprise and horror on his face at the thought that his money would, one day, all go.

Kermit was about to say something comforting when the half-naked young man came in with a tray containing the ginger beer. But as Malcolm looked again, he was almost certain that the young man had nothing on at all, the way the light now fell on him.

In this morning light, too, Kermit looked a good deal older, and crosser: he looked about twenty-two.

The young undressed man did not seem to know how to talk, but he poured and filled with ice the ginger beer in a professional and efficient manner.

Kermit kept looking irritably from Malcolm to the young servant, and from the young servant to Malcolm, and finally the midget said:

"Your *father* probably would not approve of my introducing you to a morning servant, but I feel your education could be extended, as does Professor Cox, so therefore I introduce you to O'Reilly Morgan. O'Reilly—Malcolm."

O'Reilly Morgan, the morning servant, nodded politely and

said *pleased* and *great morning* and Malcolm began to get up to shake hands, but Kermit shook his head at him, meaning that would not be necessary and pray keep his seat.

"Wouldn't O'Reilly Morgan care to have some ginger beer with us?" Malcolm inquired when the servant had gone out of the room.

Kermit swallowed some of the beer very fast and choked a little. Then frowning severely, he said quickly:

"Another time, perhaps. Just now I have to explain the very bad news to you about Laureen. And I don't want *him* to hear," and Kermit gestured in the direction of the kitchen and O'Reilly.

Kermit rapped vigorously on his chair arm, for Malcolm's attention had begun to wander a little.

"I *say,* I want you to give me your undivided attention," Kermit said. "I have a very important thing to communicate, and I don't want to shout."

"But what is it?" Malcolm leaned forward, and he felt again that he was beginning life.

"I must tell you how Laureen left me," Kermit cried, and he was very pale, as pale as if he had said he had killed her.

"You saw her last time just before the act, so to speak, and just when I thought she loved me the most. She's betrayed me, you see, from the first, and at last, she has betrayed me completely by leaving."

"She discovered who you were, then?" Malcolm asked, eager to understand.

"Who I *was?*" Kermit's voice shook.

"I mean . . . I . . . ." Malcolm faltered.

"Say exactly *what* you mean," Kermit cried, and he stood up, and in doing so, Malcolm saw to his further confusion that Kermit was scarcely any taller standing up than when he had been sitting down. Malcolm's look of surprise only increased, if anything, Kermit's ill-temper.

"Say exactly what you are thinking. I command it!" Kermit said.

"I only meant"—Malcolm winced—"she discovered at last—well, as Mr. Cox says, that you are a . . ."

"A midget! A midget!" Kermit roared. "Is that what the old pederast calls me behind my back?"

"Old *what*?" Malcolm cried, but his question was drowned in a loud crash, that of Kermit's throwing to the floor the entire tray containing the ginger beer bottles.

O'Reilly quickly entered the room, but as quickly retreated. Kermit had, however, sat down again and was weeping quietly, but with a modicum of control.

Malcolm came over to where the little man sat, but the latter vociferated at him:

"Don't touch me! I don't want pity from my *calumniators*!"

"You use such difficult words this morning," Malcolm complained, almost weeping himself.

Suddenly Kermit seized Malcolm's hand, and said in an imploring voice: "Why did she do it, Malcolm, when she was all I had?"

Malcolm wished to say something consoling, but he was afraid that he would again bring out the wrong word at such a dramatic moment.

O'Reilly again entered the room, this time wearing a kimono, and carrying a small tray with a medicine bottle. He handed Kermit a tiny pill, which the little man took perfunctorily, and swallowed, refusing the water the servant proffered him. O'Reilly immediately withdrew again.

"Oh, I hadn't loved Laureen in months," Kermit went on, steadier now. "She had lost her sparkle, and she almost disgusted me at times. But I had got so used to her and her waiting on me. I will not pretend about myself. I had come to expect her help, Malcolm. Her going away has meaning in the economic realm!"

Malcolm nodded soberly. Then wanting to say something encouraging, the boy said: "Kermit, you don't have the *voice* of a midget: you have the voice of a very young man."

Kermit's mouth opened slowly and closed, but he did not appear to have heard the compliment. He continued: "When Laureen left me last night, I seemed suddenly to have reached my majority in age. I realized that I was beginning life at last. Alone, as everybody is."

"And it's pretty scary," Malcolm volunteered.

Kermit scrutinized the boy slowly in the manner of one who is seeing him for the first time.

"We are both alone," Kermit mused. "How fortunate, after all, that Professor Cox exists and that he brought us together. We are both in an impossible situation."

"Certainly *I* am," Malcolm affirmed.

"But why you more than I?" Kermit was put out with the boy.

"You have something," Malcolm told him. "Talents. Look at your art, and your chair-making. And your marriage, which means you know women. I have nothing. I can do nothing. All I have is the memory of my father. My father—"

"Shit on your father!" Kermit cried at him.

Malcolm stood up mechanically, white with terror, and trembling all over.

There was a total silence in the room.

Kermit got up slowly and came over to Malcolm. His head reached only to the boy's waist and prevented him, humiliatingly enough, from speaking directly to Malcolm's face: his words, in fact, addressed themselves to his navel. Kermit could only tug at the tall boy's trouser legs.

"Malcolm," he cried, "you must forget I ever said it!"

Malcolm moved away from him, and sat down in a straight-back chair some feet away from where the midget was now left standing alone.

"You must listen to me, and you must forgive me." The voice of the midget came hollow and distant like something heard in a deserted subway station.

Malcolm tapped on the wood of the chair with his index finger.

"You must listen to my apology, dear Malcolm," Kermit pleaded, and he had quit crying.

"How can I ever listen to you again?" Malcolm finally spoke. "And how can I forgive you? To have said *that* about my father. This is the last straw of what can happen to me. I must pack and leave the city today. Why I have stayed this long here I don't know. And on a bench to boot."

"Listen to my apology at least," Kermit begged, and he actually raced over to where Malcolm was sitting so stiffly, and pulled savagely on Malcolm's jacket.

"You have no right to desert me," Kermit protested. "We're under the same star!"

"Is this some of Mr. Cox's astrology now?" Malcolm wondered bitterly.

"Malcolm, try to put yourself in my place. I have just given up my entire world by admitting who I really am. And I'm depending on you so. I have nobody else to depend on!"

"A likely story coming from a man who insults the dead," Malcolm said.

"I *apologize*. I apologize from the heart. Don't I know that your father was a princely type, judging by the son. Don't I see breeding and culture in every line of your face."

Malcolm nodded slightly.

"Then don't torture me any further, and forgive me."

"I don't know whether I can forgive you or not, Kermit. I don't know what my father would have done under the circumstances. If you had just said *damn his hide* or *to hell with him,* that would have been terrible enough!" And Malcolm again shivered with horror.

"I meant really nothing but irritation, not irritation against you and certainly not against your father."

"Very well, then, Kermit, you are forgiven for this once," Malcolm said.

Kermit pressed the boy's shoulder in a token of gratitude.

"Laureen! Laureen!" Kermit began muttering now, walking about the studio, and tapping his forehead from time to time. "Did I tell you who she ran away with?" Kermit inquired suddenly.

"She ran off with somebody?" Malcolm inquired.

"How else would she go!" Kermit thundered, some of his old anger coming back. "She ran off with a Japanese wrestler . . ."

Malcolm lowered his head, too tired now to take in any more of the complex events of the world. But after a moment he found the strength to inquire:

"Was he—the Japanese wrestler—also a *small* man?"

Kermit gazed at Malcolm for an interminable length of time, before replying: "He was the usual size for a man," and he spoke with great dryness and restraint.

"But Laureen will *eventually* return to you." Malcolm offered this weak consolation.

"Not Laureen," Kermit said. "No, I was only her prehusband, her breaking-in man. Now she has gone on to the real thing, as she said when she left. She's gone on to the—well, why not say it in front of children—" He spoke almost to himself. "She's gone on to the real equipment!"

And Kermit became plunged into the deepest gloom.

Address No. 3

The third address from Professor Cox had been written with a flourish of the pen which swooped down on the margin of the pale green paper like a finger of warning. It said merely:

Madame Girard
The Château

"But it doesn't tell where," Malcolm had exclaimed in his hotel suite.

Going out into the street, he had summoned a cab, and consulted with the driver concerning the address. The driver had immediately recognized it, to Malcolm's relief, and told the boy that it was the *best address,* perhaps the only *real* address in the city, and certainly the only one for high-livers, he told Malcolm, with a slight note of gravity in his voice.

A footman at the Château opened a white door on the boy, and Malcolm was taken immediately upward in a green and gold elevator which smelled strongly of patchouli and rose water.

The footman directed Malcolm, when he had alighted from the elevator, to a very narrow but very tall door, which looked more like a linen chute than an entrance. On the door, showing unmistakably it was the right one, was a message written on thick letter paper:

> *Malcolm:*
> *You Are Expected:*
> *Madame Girard.*

The footman said good night, and disappeared into the elevator.

Malcolm opened the door, and as he did so pushed his face into that of a young man in a Texas hat.

"You're *Malcolm*!" the young man, who had a very flushed face, and who was carrying a tall iced drink, said.

"How did you know me?" Malcolm wondered, but the young man began pulling him up an additional staircase, without replying to his question.

"Madame Girard is demanding a settlement from her husband," the young man informed him, tinkling the ice in his drink. "You're just in time for the evening performance."

Malcolm and the young man now entered a room almost as large as a cathedral.

Madame Girard herself faced them. She was dressed in a riding outfit, and her riding whip lay at her feet, together with several bottles, some empty, some half full. Her face was scratched, so that one would have suspected she had ridden through brambles, and her makeup was smeared so unevenly across her face and mouth that she resembled a clown more than a woman. Malcolm wished immediately that the beautiful riding habit which Madame Girard was wearing could have been bestowed on Kermit, for he was sure the midget would have looked better in it than Madame Girard.

"Who admitted this child?" Madame Girard demanded, picking up a glass of plain vodka.

Mr. Girard, her husband, a short man of middle years with

a distinguished brow, now came forward to explain to his wife:

"Professor Cox called up and asked if this young man could not be received."

Mr. Girard bowed to Malcolm and went to take his hand, but Malcolm had got both his own hands so tightly enmeshed in his trouser pockets—for the suit he was wearing was an old one which his father had picked out for him some time back, and it was becoming too small—that he was unable to return Mr. Girard's greeting and handclasp.

"And who gave *you* leave, sir, to accept invitations by proxy for me?" Madame Girard demanded of her husband. "I have a great mind to take proceedings against you, with reference to the matter which we discussed earlier in the evening!"

"Please try to be more hospitable, Doddy," Mr. Girard addressed his wife.

"Don't use pet names for me in front of strangers," Madame Girard cautioned her husband.

"Sit down please a moment," Madame Girard commanded Malcolm, and she went up close to him to get a better look.

As Malcolm looked hastily about the great glass room, beyond which one could catch glimpses of the ocean and the lights of cities, he caught sight of at least ten young men who were all seated on identical straight-back chairs—all facing Madame Girard, the sole member of her sex in the room—and all silent, like a mute chorus.

"Are all these gentlemen friends of Mr. Cox?" Malcolm said in a loud voice, for he did not feel at all comfortable in such a charged atmosphere. Everybody laughed at his remark—the ten young men laughing together very much like a chorus—all except Mr. Girard, who looked down at the carpet.

"Why is it you are not entering into the spirit of the party?" Madame Girard asked her husband. "Do you want me to begin proceedings against you at once?"

Mr. Girard put his pipe into his mouth without looking away from the carpet.

Malcolm said in his same loud voice: "I had no idea it was going to be like this."

"What is *it*?" Madame Girard demanded.

"Your gathering or party or whatever you call it," Malcolm replied. He was not impressed with Madame Girard or her friends, the young men, and he showed it.

"We are here for the sole purpose of considering taking proceedings against my husband"—Madame Girard spoke gravely—"and I think I can do this quite properly without comments from the newly arrived."

"Perhaps Mr. Girard may want a divorce first," Malcolm said, and again there was a chorus of laughter from the young men seated on the chairs, and Mr. Girard himself this time smiled from behind his pipe.

"As you may not know," Malcolm began, addressing himself to everyone present, and still employing his loud voice, "Mr. Cox, the well-known astrologer, is introducing me to all of his friends this year in the hopes that I may be a little less inclined to be lonely."

"That follows." Madame Girard tasted her vodka loudly.

"You must drink a *great* deal, Madame Girard," Malcolm said, a note of genuine worry in his voice, and there were again cries of laughter, but greatly muffled this time, while Mr. Girard bit his pipe and looked away toward a row of vases all filled with fresh garnet roses.

"What was it you said?" Madame Girard inquired, a kind of stunned craftiness in her voice, like one who must discover the precise detail which will convict her enemy.

"I think you are intoxicated, madame," Malcolm said.

The laughter from the young men now became unrestrained.

"Do you realize in whose home you are?" Madame Girard said in a breathless voice.

And in still lower tones: "And do you realize who *I* am?"

Malcolm nodded, and said: "This is the third place I've visited at Mr. Cox's request"—and he turned to face everybody in the room—"but I can't say it is the most pleasant or comfortable of the three."

"Hear him?" Madame Girard cried, standing up now. "He's a critic, not a guest. And not only a critic, but a spy! A spy of

Mr. Cox's, that's it . . . Throw him out! *Throw* him *out*!"

"Doddy, *dear*," Mr. Girard begged her, walking over to his wife and putting his hand on her arm gently.

Madame Girard sat down quickly, perhaps because she was beginning to lose her balance rather than because she wished to obey her husband.

"I believe I have heard mention of your *father*." Mr. Girard changed the topic of conversation, addressing Malcolm directly.

"He's a spy from old Mr. Cox!" Madame Girard began again, for she did not like the topic of conversation to be changed without her giving the cue.

A faint tittering from the young men came and went.

"You really knew my father!" Malcolm was all ears, but he did not say this with quite the enthusiasm he might have shown a few days earlier. Malcolm suddenly felt—even as he spoke to Mr. Girard—that the image of his father was slightly blurred in his own memory, and so he sipped the drink of vodka which a servant had just handed him.

"I do not think your father exists," Madame Girard cried, lifting her glass again. "I have *never* thought he did."

Malcolm swallowed hard, then opened his mouth to say something.

"And what is more"—Madame Girard continued to hold the floor—"*nobody* thinks he exists, or ever did exist."

"That's . . . that's . . . blasphemy . . . or a thing above it!" Malcolm cried, standing up, while Mr. Girard went up to him and attempted to say something quietly in his ear. "And this is the first time where I have ever attended a . . . a . . . *meeting*" —Malcolm chose this word after looking at all the young men on chairs—"a meeting where the person in charge was . . . drunk."

And Malcolm again turned his attention to Madame Girard as if begging her to explain the situation to him.

"As I said earlier in the evening"—Madame Girard turned her full attention now to the young men on the chairs—"I have no choice. I must take proceedings against Mr. Girard."

"Doddy, dear," Mr. Girard implored. "You do not need to take proceedings tonight . . ."

He took her glass of vodka from her and handed it to a servant who was passing by at that second.

"An enemy! A husband!" Madame Girard commented, narrowing her eyes.

Suddenly she began to weep, and all the young men except Malcolm looked very uncomfortable, while the latter, on the contrary, moved his chair a bit closer now to be able to study Madame Girard's features better.

"All my young *beauties* on their uncomfortable straight chairs —see how I am suffering!" Madame Girard implored them. "Come and comfort me, beauties," she cried, stretching out her arms to the young men.

"What a pretty face she must have under all that melted makeup," Malcolm pointed out to Mr. Girard.

Madame Girard stopped crying for a minute, and then asked her husband if he had a handkerchief, which he immediately produced from his breast pocket and handed to her.

"Wipe my face free of any blemishes," she commanded him.

"Oh, I've been through so much," Madame Girard told the room, as Mr. Girard wiped her face free of the mascara and the rouge. "Nobody knows what I have suffered! That is why I feel so often I *must* start proceedings. There ought to be a reckoning for such suffering."

"Doddy," Mr. Girard said softly to his wife.

"And with this *spy* here from Mr. Cox," she began whimpering again. "He will go directly again to that old fraud and tell him *everything* about this evening, and then Cox, blast him, will call all of his clients and tell them how I was not at the top of my form this evening."

"But why," Malcolm cried, suddenly standing up, and coming over to Madame Girard, who seemed surprised and perhaps frightened that he drew so close to her, "why *did* Mr. Cox send me here?"

"Why?" Madame Girard thundered at him. "You mean you are actually as stupid as everybody says you are! *Why?* Have I not given you the reason a score of times this evening? Yes, it is true, what everybody says about you, you have no mind. But you are Mr. Cox's spy, whether you know it or not. For he must have information at any cost . . . And to think I am not in top form!"

She now wept uncontrolledly.

Mr. Girard was so upset that as a special concession to Madame Girard he now brought her a small glass of French champagne, which she sipped, while he assiduously dried her tears with his handkerchief.

Mr. Girard at the same time motioned for Madame Girard's young "beauties" to leave their straight-back chairs and gather round her to cheer her.

Madame Girard smiled faintly when she saw the young men surrounding her in a circle, in the center of which now stood Malcolm.

"Why? Why"—Madame Girard turned to her husband—"did you spoil this beautiful evening by introducing a spy in our midst?" and she pointed again at Malcolm.

"You are not going to order me out then like Estel Blanc?" Malcolm asked, despondency and gloominess in his voice.

"Estel Blanc," Madame Girard cried, stung to the quick. "Oh, merciful God!" and she burst again into weeping.

"You should have *never* mentioned his name to her." Mr. Girard was both reproving and apologetic. "She fears him more than anybody else."

"You see," Madame Girard explained, when she had recovered from her new fit of tears, "this child knows only the worst people, and knows, indeed, only my enemies. Oh, make him leave, Girard, for pity's sake, make him leave."

"Doddy, remember your long years of position," Mr. Girard begged her. "Remember *society*, if you will not remember your position."

"Oh, it's so hard to bear one's burdens sometimes," she said, drinking more of her champagne. "And we don't need him." She pointed to Malcolm. "Don't I have my beauties already?" Here she recognized with a peremptory nod the young men.

"Why aren't *they* enough. Why must we have a paid informer in the shape of this brainless, mindless, but—" and here Madame Girard paused as if seeing Malcolm for the very first time —"this very *beautiful* young boy?"

"Perhaps we should all drink to Madame Girard!" Malcolm cried, astonished at her lightning change of attitude toward him, and he raised his glass, and even as he did so, everybody could see that he was quite drunk himself.

"My dear, dear young friend," Madame Girard cried. "Oh, thank you."

All the young men and Mr. Girard now raised their glasses, and Malcolm, too, with some difficulty raised his again, got his glass to his lips, and drained it. A servant immediately replenished his glass for him, at a sign from Madame Girard.

"Leave Mr. Cox." Madame Girard addressed Malcolm. "Be my own, and not his."

"Let us all drink again to Madame Girard," Mr. Girard cried nervously, and the young men all gathered round him, and some patted him on the back, relieved at the breaking of the tension in the room.

"Do you know, my young, my very young dear friend, the company you are keeping?" Madame Girard stood up now, seized one of the garnet roses from a vase, and in a twinkling had pushed it into Malcolm's hitherto unused lapel.

Malcolm kissed Madame Girard lightly on her cheek, reeling toward her.

"Answer my question, wonderful young man," Madame Girard demanded, and she seemed almost sober. "Do you know the company you keep? Do you know, dear boy, what Mr. Cox himself is?" she cried.

"Why, a pederast, of course." Malcolm reeled, his piercing loud voice a bit shaky and thick.

"What!" everybody cried at once, and the young men stared at one another in open-mouthed astonishment and disbelief.

"What word did I hear?" Madame Girard exclaimed, a bemused smile lifting her cheeks.

"I don't intend to repeat myself!" Malcolm cried, draining

his glass. "My father never did! . . . Hurrah!" he shouted, and suddenly he fell to the floor in a sitting posture.

Madame Girard rose from her chair, pushing aside the ten "beauties" and her husband, went swiftly over to where Malcolm lay slowly sinking into her thick carpet, and like a woman who has decided at last to come to terms with her own fresh decision, she bent low over the boy, a complete change of will and soul in her face. She stopped again, as if seeing him for the first time; she held her hands to her breast, the change in her mind registering itself now in her heart:

"You are a real prince, Malcolm," she cried. "Oh, forgive me. An authentic—"

And Madame Girard muffled the word she was saying by kissing him vociferously on his hair as he lay staring at her from his sitting posture.

"Royalty!" she cried, pointing out Malcolm to the other guests staring anxiously at them both. "Royalty."

A visit from the magnate

~~~~~~

Malcolm passed the next few days talking from time to time with Mr. Cox, who stood as usual before the boy, while the latter was seated on his bench, and writing down his "conversations" with the personages of the addresses.

Mr. Cox agreed that Address No. 4 should not be given to Malcolm until he had completely digested the scenes and significance of the first three addresses.

Then, shortly after this, one late evening, Malcolm was surprised when, as he lay in his large canopied bed listening to the different seashells which his father had bought him when they had been on their travels, he heard, through the incrustations of the shells, the uncommon sound of the telephone ringing.

Answering it, he was still more surprised to hear the voice of Mr. Girard, who was, he said, telephoning him from the lobby of the hotel.

"Can I see you, Malcolm?"

Mr. Girard was sober and self-possessed, as always, for although he may have been accustomed to consume as much alcohol as Madame Girard, his strong will resisted all stimulants.

It was Malcolm who was not at ease, for it was the first time anybody had ever telephoned to see him since the days his father often dropped in unexpectedly from Denver or San Francisco from a business deal. Helplessly listening to Mr. Girard on the phone, Malcolm was not able to reply at once, owing to his confusion.

Mr. Girard, hearing only Malcolm's breathing on the other end of the wire, and no response to his inquiry, apologized again for the lateness of his call, but repeated his wish to see the boy.

"I don't see why you can't see me, if you don't mind seeing me just dressed in my bathrobe," Malcolm finally said.

"I will be right up, then," Mr. Girard told him.

In Malcolm's suite, Mr. Girard looked much younger and more handsome, but also, oddly enough, more careworn and worried than he had in the Château.

He seemed at home in the large faded elegance of Malcolm's hotel suite, and Malcolm immediately offered him a tumbler of ice water.

"I felt somehow we were of the same station in life," Mr. Girard began, and he took a seat on the divan, "—even though I am so much older than you. How old are you, Malcolm?" he wondered.

Malcolm swallowed, and moved his fingers, like one who is counting.

"Fifteen, sir," the boy replied.

Mr. Girard looked at him hesitatingly.

"That is, sir, I will be in December, I think," Malcolm added.

"I see," Mr. Girard said. "And it is now June, isn't it? . . . Well, you see, I am thirty-seven, so that I am easily old enough to be your father."

"Yes, you are, I see," Malcolm answered. "My father, however, looked older, though perhaps stronger, than you. He looked nearly forty."

"I hope I have not disturbed you," Mr. Girard continued. "But my coming is dictated by an emergency."

"Nothing serious?" Malcolm expressed concern. "Madame Girard has not taken ill or died?"

"Madame Girard is home sleeping in her private wing of the Château," Mr. Girard replied. "I simply came here to make a very unusual suggestion to you, and I hope you will hear me out. I have come, though—I must make clear—on my own volition, despite the fact that Madame Girard herself ordered me to come."

Mr. Girard wiped his forehead with his pocket handkerchief.

"You seem, Malcolm, so close to me in general background and point of view, and Madame Girard has taken such an imme- diate and violent fancy to you, also, that we wondered"—and here Mr. Girard took out a small silver box which contained some pastilles and popped one hurriedly into his mouth—"we wondered if you would care to come with us to our country house for the summer. Everything would be taken care of, of course, and you would not have to give up your hotel suite, as I would be glad to take all responsibility with regard to that . . ."

"Why, I am speechless with surprise at your generosity," Malcolm exclaimed, and he got up and walked about the room for a minute or two.

"Would you care to listen to one of my seashells for a mo- ment?" Malcolm offered one of the larger shells.

"Are you paying close attention to what I have proposed to you, Malcolm?" Mr. Girard was a bit grave at that moment, and he did not accept the proffered seashell.

"Oh, yes, sir, very close attention," Malcolm replied. "No- body has ever invited me anywhere, you see, except my father. I have not been out of this hotel, mind you, except to go occasionally to other hotels—that is, until I met Mr. Cox."

Mr. Girard tapped somewhat impatiently on the wooden end of the divan.

"You will make both me and my wife very happy if you will come," Mr. Girard said in the manner of a man concluding an agreement. "And we may expect you, then?"

"But I would have to leave all of my new friends!" Malcolm cried out.

"Your new friends?" Mr. Girard said with the surprise of a

man who hears something totally unforeseen and something uncalled for, to boot.

"Kermit Raphaelson and Mr. Cox, especially," Malcolm informed him. "I don't count Estel Blanc really—not as a friend —though perhaps in twenty years, as he said himself, that might be a possibility."

"I don't recognize these people except by name." Mr. Girard was somewhat withdrawn now. "You see, Malcolm, I am often gone, and don't always get to know my wife's friends. Often, in fact, I've never heard their names and then returning late to the Château from a long trip, I meet them face to face for the first time. And often I never see them again after our first meeting."

"You don't seem to care, then, for the friends of others," Malcolm observed.

"Well, dear Malcolm, I won't deny that I have never liked any of my wife's friends. You are the first."

"You mean, you really are in earnest about me?" Malcolm was surprised.

"Why, of course I am in earnest!" Mr. Girard replied a bit hotly. "I am always in earnest."

"But you see, Mr. Girard, sir, you do not understand," Malcolm assured him. "Until I met Mr. Cox on the bench my whole life was just this hotel suite. There was nothing much to it. And now suddenly, invitations from everywhere, people ringing me up at midnight. There is almost *too* much of it."

And Malcolm went up and shook Mr. Girard's hand, who, not being exactly ready for such a display of etiquette, stood up, and his sudden raising of his knees pushed the boy away from him, so that the latter came close to losing his balance.

Mr. Girard remained standing in this awkward posture.

"I feel, Mr. Girard, sir," Malcolm said, recovering his composure, "that life is actually *beginning*."

"I feel very much the same as you, Malcolm," Mr. Girard replied, "and although my life is over in the sense of a beginning, I seem to see it starting all over again in you. Perhaps it is because you are like a son to me. But as I said earlier in the evening, I believe that you are in my own general situation and in my part of the world."

"Thanks to my father," Malcolm said.

"No, not thanks to your father," Mr. Girard assured him. "Thanks to you. It is to you we all look, and not your father."

"That is very hard for me to believe, Mr. Girard," Malcolm said.

"What is hard?" Mr. Girard questioned, concern written all over his face.

"That you place such a high estimate on me, sir. You see, my difficulty is I can hardly place any estimate on myself. I hardly feel I exist."

"You feel you don't exist?" Mr. Girard weighed the boy's words.

"That's right. And when other people pay so much attention to me all at once, I feel something has gone wrong somewhere . . ."

"Everybody is fond of you," Mr. Girard said. "At least we are, and I am certain everybody else must be likewise."

"Thank you, Mr. Girard, sir," and Malcolm looked down at the gold embroidery on his dressing gown.

"Then you will accept the invitation, Malcolm?"

"I will be happy to *accept* it, Mr. Girard."

"Please call me by my first name, although I am more than twenty years older than you."

"What is your first name?" Malcolm wondered somewhat bashfully, hesitating to ask such a question of so great a man.

"Girard," Mr. Girard said.

"But that is your last name, sir?"

"My last name and my first name are the same."

"You mean you are—"

"Girard *Girard,* that is right. When I was a young man, it was very hard to bear, but now that I'm old, I like it."

"You are a very likeable old man," Malcolm affirmed.

"I felt perhaps that you admired me, and that is one of the reasons I wanted you to come with us. My wife, however, is very much the partisan of you."

"She is?" Malcolm swallowed, hesitating on the word *partisan*. "Thank her, please."

"Now when do you think you can make your little visit?" Girard said.

"Oh, I can't come," Malcolm replied firmly.

"What?" Girard said, a note of imperious anger in his voice, so that he assumed his full character as billionaire and magnate in one change of expression.

"It has nothing to do with you," Malcolm said calmly, walking up and down the room.

Mr. Girard drank all of the ice water in his glass, opened his *pastille* box with a snap, looked into it, took nothing out this time, and closed it with another snap.

Malcolm was somewhat taken aback at how fierce Girard looked at that moment.

"I can't leave the bench," Malcolm told him. "And I don't think I can just walk out on Kermit and Mr. Cox."

"Well, bring them along with you"—Mr. Girard expressed some relief—"if that's all!"

"I don't even know whether I can call you Girard, sir," Malcolm went on.

"Because of my extreme age?" Girard wondered.

"I don't know what it is, sir," Malcolm said. "Maybe because to address you so sounds . . . *insubordinate*, I believe they say."

Girard Girard stopped, then said: "Well, who the devil cares what you call me. Call me anything or nothing, but come!"

Mr. Girard tried to smile and look pleasant.

"You see," Malcolm continued, "I'm terribly afraid of leaving here where I'm always alone, and waiting, and going to where people may demand me at all hours . . ."

"No one will demand anything of you that you don't want to give," Mr. Girard said patiently, and Malcolm felt that the great man's patience was rapidly diminishing.

"I must turn down your kind invitation." Malcolm summoned all his bravery.

"There must be some other reason which you are not giving."

"No, *Girard*"—Malcolm made the effort with his name—
"there is none. I can't explain the reason except that it has
something to do with the bench, Mr. Cox's instructions, and
also my new friend, Kermit, who, by the way, must be very hurt
that he has never been invited to the Château to meet Madame
Girard, and of course, sir, you . . ."

"I see," Girard said, ignoring nearly everything Malcolm
had said. However, he made no motion to leave.

"I want to please you very much," Malcolm said after a long
silence. "And Madame Girard, too, though I don't know why
I want to please her, except I do."

"Then you'll reconsider?" Mr. Girard cried in a loud voice.

"I *want* to come," Malcolm told him. "But I'm afraid I
can't."

"What then are you afraid of?" Girard now thundered.

"I believe, sir, as I said, it has something to do with leaving
the bench."

"Don't call me *sir*!" Girard commanded with icy severity.
"And what in hell is this bench . . ."

"The bench . . . from where I get all the addresses. Where,
in fact, I got yours, Girard Girard!"

Girard knitted his brow.

"My head is still spinning from all the addresses, those past
and to come . . . And there are dozens more yet. Perhaps
hundreds. You must give me time, Girard Girard."

"But what in thunderation is this bench?" Girard was less
angry now.

"It's below the hotel where I always waited for my father to
come home."

Mr. Girard's mouth opened and shut.

"I had hardly spoken to anybody since my father's disappearance and/or death when Mr. Cox tried to introduce me to life
and people."

"Mr. Cox!" Girard threw up his hands.

"My father's death has left me—"

"Exactly!" Girard interrupted. "Going to the country with us
is precisely what you need."

But there was now no conviction or feeling in the billionaire's voice. Instead there was hesitancy, and sadness.

"We will be your father and your friends," Girard said finally. He went up to Malcolm and was about to put his hand on the boy's shoulder, when, changing his mind, he allowed his hand merely to fall downward like a benediction.

"At least consider it," Girard said.

"I will," Malcolm replied.

"And don't look so sad," Girard admonished him. "I never knew, of course, about the bench or I would have been more careful about what I said."

"No apology is needed, Girard Girard, sir."

"Thank you," the elder man replied.

"And I am so grateful for your visit," Malcolm went on. "Please don't tell anybody what I have said here to you. You see, Mr. Cox knows everything about me, though I have not told him a thing. He just knows it. As an astrologer, you see . . ."

Girard did not reply to this, but instead went on to talk about Malcolm's possible visit. "You must inform Madame Girard as soon as possible. We hope to leave any day now, and we must have you in the bargain."

"I will give it my undivided attention," Malcolm said.

"That's right, that is what you should do," Girard said. "Sleep on it, as they say."

Malcolm yawned.

"Good night," Girard said. "And remember, you are ours."

Malcolm said good night and opened the door for Girard onto the long gray-carpeted hall. "Thank you, sir, and a very good night."

"There is no more for me to do"

Malcolm had slept until past two o'clock in the afternoon because of the lateness of Girard Girard's visit, so that any meeting with Mr. Cox on the bench did not seem feasible. Malcolm did not reach the bench, in fact, until nearly four o'clock, and by then he sensed that the astrologer had come and gone.

Malcolm walked resolutely therefore to Kermit's, rehearsing as he went the exact words he would use to tell the midget of his last night's visitor.

It was no real surprise for Malcolm, however, on entering the studio to find both Kermit and Mr. Cox engaged in what appeared to be a very close *tête-à-tête.* They both looked somewhat guilty on seeing Malcolm, perhaps because they were then talking about him.

"Where were *you* at the appointed hour?" Mr. Cox assailed Malcolm. "I waited for you for nearly ten minutes!"

"Are you speaking of my not being at the bench?" Malcolm brought out somewhat indifferently, because he felt so much stronger owing to Girard Girard's call.

"And who else around here has a bench?" Mr. Cox cried.

"I can't ever remember having kept regular hours or appointments with *anybody*," Malcolm said, and he recalled at that moment that Madame Girard had used the word "royalty" with reference to him only a few nights ago. He therefore fancied that his speech and manner at this moment must seem royal also to Kermit and Mr. Cox.

But both Mr. Cox and Kermit were looking at him with cold and even critical eyes.

"I had such a late visitor last night." Malcolm addressed his words now to Kermit. "And I made certain arrangements at that time also for you, Kermit," he added for the midget.

"A busy boy," Kermit said, somewhat cool, though with no real irony.

"Are you attempting to tell us by gesture and word that you no longer need us?" Mr. Cox said, ignoring the news of Malcolm's late visitor, and going to the bottom of Malcolm's psychology of the moment.

Malcolm was surprised at Mr. Cox's unpleasant tone. He had known Mr. Cox was not very kind or warm-hearted, but he had not known until now that his tone could be so nasty.

"Who have you been recommending me to?" Kermit ignored Mr. Cox's question, and went back to Malcolm's visitor. "I can't wait to know."

"I had, as I said, an unusual visitor," Malcolm began again. "In fact, I should say that I had a visitor for the first time since my father disappeared and/or died. My father was my only visitor before, not counting bootblacks and hotel managers."

"How you do repeat yourself, dear Malcolm." Mr. Cox raised his eyes to the ceiling, and Kermit cleared his throat delicately.

"What a cold contemptuous person you can be at times, Mr. Cox," Malcolm remarked.

"Hear! hear!" Mr. Cox cried, and Kermit smiled broadly, for Mr. Cox was almost never criticized to his face, though he received nothing but criticism behind his back.

"Mr. Cox was also denounced at the Château the other night by Madame Girard," Malcolm informed them.

"My being denounced by Madame Girard is hardly news to me." Mr. Cox took this up: "A woman who owes all her success to me naturally must defame me frequently in order for her to feel that she exists in her own right at all."

"She doesn't exist . . . in her own right, then?" Malcolm was concerned.

"Well, how did she strike *you,* dear Malcolm?" Mr. Cox interrogated.

"But I don't want to tell you about my evening with Madame Girard this afternoon," Malcolm interrupted. "That might have been all right for a morning on the bench, but—"

"Then what do you want to tell about?" the astrologer inquired.

"Why, his visitor, of course, you old—" but Kermit checked himself before he said the word, laughing at the same time, perhaps because he saw that he had at last a supporter in Malcolm against Mr. Cox's long tyranny.

"Perhaps I should save my story until Kermit and I are alone," Malcolm ventured.

"You will tell what it is you have to tell here and now, and we'll have no more of this young-person coyness and drooling about," Mr. Cox commanded.

"I am not at all frightened of your manner," Malcolm told Mr. Cox bravely.

"Everything you have—everything you've even been discussing for days now," Mr. Cox began, "you owe to me. Try to remember that when you feel proud and free!"

"Are we to hear Malcolm's adventure, or are we to discuss our indebtedness to you, sir?" Kermit addressed Mr. Cox.

"What happened," Malcolm said without any further delay, "is that Girard Girard came to see me in person last night, at midnight."

Both Mr. Cox and Kermit were too thunderstruck to reply immediately.

When not even Mr. Cox could bring himself to comment on this intelligence, Kermit, after some struggle, brought out: "Do you fully realize the honor which has been paid you, Malcolm?"

"Honor?" Malcolm replied, seriously trying to understand now.

"How could he realize, *fully* or *at all*!" Mr. Cox said, flushed and irritable.

"Malcolm," Kermit exclaimed, going over to where the boy was seated, and taking his hand vigorously into his, like one who is to communicate with the deaf and dumb. "Girard Girard is a billionaire, a maker of presidents, a friend of royalty—a MAGNATE!"

"A friend of royalty?" Malcolm caught at this one phrase.

"Wined and dined by crowned heads, an African explorer, and a poet!"

"A poet?" Malcolm was puzzled and not very much interested.

"*The* man of his period," Kermit concluded.

Then turning to the astrologer, the midget said hopelessly: "Professor Cox, he is not impressed."

"Well, how could you expect him to be?" Mr. Cox was very put out. "He's had only three addresses, and this was a plunge I had not expected him to take at all. Perhaps never . . . Girard Girard! . . . Oh, it's quite premature . . ."

"You're angry Girard came," Malcolm cried, standing up, for he felt suddenly he had been betrayed.

"Why, he calls Girard by his first name," Kermit noted with stupefaction.

"Don't be ridiculous, Malcolm." Mr. Cox scolded Malcolm for having suggested they were angry. "Angry at *you*! Be seated at once," and the astrologer made a snorting kind of sound.

"For God's sake, tell us what happened," Kermit said, disbelief still struggling with amazement.

"Why . . . nothing happened," Malcolm said, feeling now almost that perhaps Mr. Cox was right, and that he understood nothing, and that if Girard's coming had not been exactly a dream, it had not added up to anything more than his arrival and departure.

"You mean Girard Girard simply looked in on you for no purpose," Mr. Cox exclaimed.

"It was midnight," Malcolm began, "and I was listening to my South Sea shells in my bathrobe."

"Ahem," Mr. Cox said.

"And Girard Girard was all of a sudden on the phone wanting to see me."

"I would give ten years of my life to be so honored," Kermit said.

"I told Girard Girard all about you"—Malcolm addressed Kermit now—"though, of course, I didn't describe you in *detail,* but merely said you were a young unattached man, and my best friend."

Kermit clapped his hands. "You will receive an award for that," the midget told Malcolm.

"You imbecile." Mr. Cox now turned his attention to the midget. "You sound—the both of you—like a couple of schoolgirls—all excited over the visit of a—common manipulator of the stock market."

Kermit stuck out his tongue at Mr. Cox, and turned back to Malcolm.

"It seems that both Madame Girard and Girard Girard feel they have to have me for their very own," Malcolm said, and he felt that with this sentence he had told the whole interesting story, and so he rested his hands in his lap, and was silent, expecting that his auditors would take up the conversation from there.

But when neither Mr. Cox nor Kermit added anything, but sat waiting expectantly for more, Malcolm added, by way of elucidation: "They love me, I guess, the Girards."

"Completely incredible—the whole shebang!" Mr. Cox shifted on his chair.

"You know Malcolm does not lie," Kermit told the astrologer. "But you can't stand to hear of success, of course, especially with regard to one of your own friends. Success in others is for you what hell is to a pious believer, and success is the defeat of any plans you may have for your friends."

"I don't believe the Girards could love anybody but themselves." Mr. Cox ignored Kermit. "Madame Girard can't think about anything but herself, in any case, for more than five minutes, without becoming panicky."

"They—" Malcolm continued, musing, "or rather Madame Girard through Girard Girard invited me to spend my vacation in the country with them."

"At their country estate?" Kermit cried.

"That's the place," Malcolm replied.

Even Mr. Cox was convinced by this statement, and he sat back slowly, collapsing downward until his hands touched the floor. It was all over, he knew. He had done it, he had set the ball rolling, and it had rolled further than he had ever dreamed or contemplated. Malcolm was definitely "in"—long long before he was ready, and long before Mr. Cox had seen any indication—astrologically—that Malcolm was anywhere near his goal. Malcolm had arrived, without ever having put his foot on the first rung of the ladder. He was the protégé, after an evening's talk, of the country's most powerful man.

"But do you know what has happened to you?" Kermit questioned the boy.

"Of course he does not." Mr. Cox was still acid. "But as you say, Kermit, he could not lie about it. Nobody could invent a thing this large. No, Malcolm has simply done it."

"But what have I done?" Malcolm cried.

"You've captured *them,*" Kermit shouted. "Isn't that enough for one lifetime?"

Then, remembering his conversation with Girard Girard, Malcolm said in his slow loud voice:

"But I turned the invitation down."

"What?" Kermit leaped to his feet from the chair in which he had been sitting. Malcolm shielded his face, for the little man's expression was so threatening the boy feared he was about to be attacked. But Kermit only remained frozen in his tracks with vicarious chagrin.

Mr. Cox put his hands over his eyes and bowed slightly, and then shook his head.

"But Girard Girard persuaded me at the last that one day I *must* accept," Malcolm added weakly, and Kermit and Mr. Cox gave out sighs of partial relief in the thought that all had not been won, then, only to be thrown so wantonly away.

"Malcolm should have a keeper," Mr. Cox said to Kermit. "How he has kept alive this long is a mystery, of course."

"I'm not going to their country estate without you, Kermit." It was Malcolm's turn now to stand up and tell his questioners. "I told Girard Girard that, in so many words."

Kermit did not answer, but he turned very pale, and looked away from Mr. Cox, who was observing him closely.

"I believe there is no more for me to do here," Mr. Cox said suddenly, getting up, for he could no longer conceal that he had not been prepared for Malcolm's surprise, and nothing in his own science had warned him of the event.

"Sit down, Professor Cox," Kermit fulminated. "You've played God long enough. You'll act now like other mortals . . ."

And Kermit beat on a small gong for his morning servant, forgetting that it was not morning, and that O'Reilly Morgan had gone.

"There is so much to think about," Kermit said, referring, all knew, to Malcolm's visitor. "And so much to plan."

But Mr. Cox had already gone toward the door. He had, after all, perhaps done enough for both of the young men. He hesitated with his back to them, and then taking hold of the knob, opened the door, and went out without another word.

The Girards call on Kermit

One afternoon, following a vague warning of their arrival, a Rolls drew up in front of Kermit's studio, and Madame Girard, Girard Girard, and Malcolm all got out and stood before the door.

The small figure of Kermit waited, his eyes fixed on the bolt and chain of his door: he feared these might give under the combined pressure of the three visitors outside.

They had come, of course, he knew, to take him to the country mansion. He had agreed to go—in some indefinite future—but now that he saw the sudden splendor of Madame Girard, the princely calm and command of Girard Girard, and the unbelievable youth of Malcolm, he acknowledged to himself that he could not open the door to them. He could not, he knew, be happy. The sight of such wealth and effulgence blinded him. He had intended, of course, to open the door, to receive them. O'Reilly Morgan had already made the tea, a special blend he had purchased only that morning. The entire studio had been washed down in ammonia, followed by patchouli oil and rose water (Madame Girard's *sina qua non* for habitations), and was in immaculate order. And Kermit had planned to receive Madame Girard in the style she was led to expect everywhere. Then, at the very last of the reception, Kermit had been going to tell Madame Girard calmly, even a little majestically, that other commitments would prevent him from accepting her kind invitation. She would protest, of course, but in the end would give in, regretful, and leave, while caring more for the little man than if he had accepted and gone with her.

The spectacle of the three persons outside his shabby ramshackle studio pierced his breast with such force that he felt he might fall insensible if they did not depart at once. At the same time, even if he had now desired it, he would never have had the strength to be able to lift the bolt and latch and admit them.

After a few moments, a humiliating realization crossed Kermit's brain. He saw, gradually, that Malcolm had from the first recognized his "outline" against the glass door: Malcolm had recognized him but was not letting the others know. Of course, it would have been too great an insult for Madame Girard had she known he was hiding there behind the door, and so the boy had kept silent.

Kermit could not move now, he could not even show to Malcolm that he knew the latter had recognized him. He stood there like a prisoner in stocks, helpless to run even and hide from his shame. He had deceived them, and here he stood, the shadow of his perfidy and deceit falling upon them: he had said he would go with them to the country, and now he had bolted the door against them, and had, in effect, insulted them with his contempt.

Kermit saw Malcolm's feverish and concentrated frown. Then, suddenly, he heard Malcolm's voice saying to Madame Girard: "I'm certain he *has* to be in there!"

"He has *chosen* not to see us," Madame Girard said with her haunting fear that those she really wished to know feared and avoided her.

"Perhaps something has happened to him," Girard Girard

suggested, and he went up to the door and beat loudly on the old frail glass.

Kermit drew back briefly. The sound of so much power being exerted on his door by one of the most influential living men was too upsetting to his already frayed sensibilities. The little man began slowly retreating backward into the room reserved for the cats.

He knew now that he could never go with them. He was too used to poverty, to the routine of deprivation, to his little empty life of complaint and irritations, and the final inanity when he tucked himself into his small bed. To be suddenly translated into a car with a monogram that looked like a vehicle from another civilization, to be surrounded by what was, in effect, royalty, and to see Malcolm enthroned as the favorite—he could never do this. He retreated still further back, and as he did so, the movement of his back pushed open the door, and all the cats, seeing their prison open, rushed out with cries of wildness and relief into the front room and began scratching and meowing on the pane of the tall glass door before which Madame Girard now stood.

Madame Girard gave out cries of delight when she was aware of the presence of the cats.

Malcolm pushed his face against the glass of the door, and as he did so, the lock sprang open, and they were all admitted into the studio.

Kermit, though himself invisible in the dark back part of his studio, was able to see his visitors clearly, and observed that Malcolm was near tears, calling out: "I can't go alone, Kermit, you don't know what will happen! I can't go alone! Come out, and don't be a coward."

Madame Girard now raised her voice: "Come here this instant, Kermit. I am issuing a command, do you hear me? A *command.*"

At this imperious order, Kermit felt that he could no longer stand the suspense and the pressure, and calling out to them, he said: "Go away! I can't bear the splendor of your being here!"

"What is it you can't bear?" Madame Girard cried, trying to see into the inky blackness of the studio's interior so that she could catch some short glimpse of the little man.

"I can't stand the splendor of your presence!" Kermit repeated.

"The splendor of our *presence!*" Madame Girard cried, for she feared her ears deceived her.

"Open the door to your closet, and come out at once, when I command!" she exclaimed.

"I could never, *never*," Kermit now groaned, his head pressed against the narrow door of the back room.

"The little creature is moaning!" Madame Girard commented, at which words Kermit's weeping became more audible.

"Open your door, and come out," Malcolm cried to Kermit.

Girard Girard now added his voice to those of the others, but with the calm and dignity which Kermit would have expected from so famous a man.

Worn out from his emotion, Kermit let himself slowly slip to his knees where he genuflected before the thin wooden door, which separated him from his visitors.

Madame Girard continued to knock with her soft gloved hands on the glass pane of the door, Mr. Girard offered counsel, and Malcolm urged Kermit to come *for his sake,* if for no other.

Kermit attempted several times to answer one or another of these eloquent appeals, but his voice always choked up, and no words came out.

After a wait, the three visitors went slowly away and sat in the Rolls waiting for the little man to change, perhaps, his mind.

They seemed, the three of them, to Kermit, to wait there for hours, while he never moved from his position of kneeling. Dusk fell. Then, as the night was beginning to show itself in all its black city completeness, the engine of the Rolls started and his splendid visitors motored off into the void.

"Kermit has rejected me," Madame Girard said, as they drove off.

"I'm afraid it's me he's rejected," Malcolm replied. He

looked now almost as small as Kermit from his position alone in the back seat of the Rolls. In the heavy rich-smelling leather and severe uprightness of the car, he felt that he was going to his own funeral. He was impatient to jump out and rejoin Kermit in the studio. He knew that he did not belong with "royalty" any more than Kermit had believed himself to belong with them.

Soon Malcolm began sobbing in earnest.

"Oh, no, no," Madame Girard cried, turning about and looking at him from the front seat where she sat stiffly at a distance from Girard himself, who was driving.

"I am not very manly, I suppose you are thinking." Malcolm blew his nose on his sleeve.

"I cannot *stand* emotional crises in others." Madame Girard explained her position. "This must be attended to, Girard." She turned to her husband. "Do something at once."

"We will drive and think." Her husband made the rejoinder.

"There is nothing to think." Madame Girard took this up. "Kermit has rejected all of us. He stood back there, probably staring at us as if we were odd-plumaged birds in a sanctuary."

"That was the worst thing about it," Malcolm agreed. "To see his little shadow in the glass door watching us. Too afraid to make his presence known."

"How could he be afraid—when it was only love I wanted to bring him?" Madame Girard said.

"We could telephone him, perhaps, and tell him what it is that we actually wish of him," Girard proposed. "People often cannot refuse a request when it is telephoned."

"I must also have a drink," Madame Girard said in her deepest voice.

"What of?" Malcolm asked, rather severely and loudly.

Madame Girard thought for a long time, while humming, and then said, very quickly, so that everybody jumped a bit: "Dark rum."

"Completely out of the question," Girard assured her.

"Explain the meaning of that last remark." Madame Girard addressed her husband.

"Your drinking days are over. At any rate, with me present.

I know that at night you sometimes run off and get it, or perhaps when young men come they *secret* it in to you but, on the whole, your drinking days are over."

"He pronounces my sentence of doom with the *sangfroid* of an ape," Madame Girard said. "You are an ape. It was your malign presence which frightened the midget!"

"Never use that word!" Malcolm exclaimed.

"Sir?" Madame Girard cried, turning about again to look at Malcolm.

"Kermit doesn't think he *is* a midget," Malcolm told her. "He was about to strike me one afternoon for almost *thinking* it."

"How perfectly remarkable," Madame Girard said, her mind temporarily lifted for a moment from her desire for drink. "How intensely significant."

Thinking still more, Madame Girard asked: "What *does* he think he is?"

"I feared you were going to ask that," Malcolm confessed.

Madame Girard nodded, understanding.

"I don't suppose he has quite decided what he thinks he is," Malcolm suggested.

"Perhaps, however," Girard spoke up, "if we knew what he thought he was, we would be able to persuade him to come with us."

"You could persuade nobody—*nothing*!" Madame Girard exploded, and her husband bent slightly under the vigor of her attack.

"You henpeck Girard, I observe," Malcolm commented.

Madame Girard turned her blazing mascaraed eyes with the purple puffs under them directly into the line of Malcolm's flashing teeth.

"How do I do that?" she wondered, more curious than belligerent.

"You reduce him to a smaller size than he should be," Malcolm ventured.

"I am quite a strong man, reduced or not," Girard laughed.

"He is very strong," Madame Girard agreed, looking at her

husband. "But we're off the subject," she reminded them. "We have to have Kermit or we have to go home, because Malcolm would cry himself into the hospital, should we set off for the country now."

"We *must* go to the country," Girard said. "My lungs require that air."

"You will do as you're told," Madame Girard affirmed. "Drive to the Avenue of the Temples."

"But that's far far out of our way!" Girard protested.

"Did you hear what I said?" Madame Girard demanded. "I said the Temples!"

"And with me not having been near the bench for what seems days," Malcolm sighed, almost to himself.

"I insist a phone call to Kermit is in order." Mr. Girard returned to his original idea.

"Well, there are phones in the Temples." Madame Girard gave in a bit, grudgingly.

"What *is* to become of Kermit?" Malcolm said, realizing all in a flash what the life of the little man must be.

"Beautiful small men like that go on living," Madame Girard assured him.

"How did you know he was beautiful?" Malcolm wondered.

"Silhouettes tell all," she replied.

"I thought his voice was distinguished," Girard said.

"Everything about him was distinguished." Madame Girard summarized their afternoon. "And that wonderful studio. I wish to buy it as soon as possible."

"Buy?" Girard said.

"You heard me." Madame Girard was cold now. "I must own the studio."

"I don't think it's for sale," Malcolm informed her.

"Oh, it's too beautiful, of course, but it's for sale, naturally —if I want it—it *has* to be!"

"Here are your Temples," Girard said, pointing out to them with a wave of his gloved hand the ruins of an old Japanese-style building.

The ruins struck a kind of autumnal chill in each of them.

"Where are the telephones?" It was Malcolm who spoke up at last.

"Near by," Girard assured him. "And I *will* call him."

"The Temples bring back so many memories for me," Madame Girard said in an altered voice, and she put her gloved hand over her eyes. Malcolm studied her very closely.

"Do you want your veil?" Girard asked her, looking down, unaccountably, at the floor of the car.

"Madame Girard wears a . . . *riding* veil?" Malcolm wondered, too much surprised for politeness in his voice.

"Here it is, my dear," Girard said, ignoring Malcolm's remark, and he handed Madame Girard a bluish-purple cloth, which he had taken quickly from a compartment in the car. She placed the cloth over her face immediately.

"A riding veil should prove very attention-bringing to any possible walkers at this time," Malcolm told Madame Girard.

"This veil, of course, would bring attention wherever it was displayed," she replied.

She touched it at that moment, gingerly, with her hand.

"You could be the headless huntsman," Malcolm told her.

"Texture is all," Madame Girard said, "substance nothing."

"Shall I now telephone Kermit?" Girard brought them back to the afternoon and their failure.

"By all means, use every way of persuading him," Madame Girard consented.

"You will excuse me, then, while I do so," Girard said.

Both Malcolm and Madame Girard bowed to him, and he went off in the direction of the Japanese Temples.

Girard Girard was gone such a short time that Madame Girard had scarcely spoken ten words to Malcolm through the blue veil which now cut her off from the world. Malcolm, however, had decided that her veiled appearance went very well with the Temples and the melancholy of the light, and was about to tell her this when Girard Girard returned, looking, Malcolm thought, somewhat happier than when he had left. He looked assuaged.

"It's good news I bring," Girard said.

"Let *us* decide its quality," Madame Girard told him. "Come into the car and tell *only* what happened. If comments or adjectives are to be supplied, we shall do so."

"I see," Girard said, and smiling, he took his position at the wheel.

"Was I gone long?" Girard wondered suddenly.

"You were gone the normal length of time," Madame Girard replied.

"I seemed to be gone a long time," he explained.

"It was not long," Malcolm told him.

"I think the reason for the seeming length of my stay was that I had to talk with a man named Professor Cox."

"No!" broke from both Malcolm and Madame Girard.

"Mr. Cox is everywhere," Madame Girard said, shaking her head, and she lifted her veil momentarily. Malcolm decided that he liked Madame Girard better with her veil on than off, and was about to tell her so when Girard went on: "Professor Cox was very evasive."

"How could he be straightforward?" Madame Girard inquired.

"He was, in any case, very firm," Girard admitted.

"Well, he is firmly evasive, we might say," Madame Girard commented.

"I asked him naturally for Kermit, since I was not able to recognize the voice which answered the phone."

"Continue," Madame Girard commanded her husband.

" 'This is Mr. Cox,' the voice then identified itself. And I asked, 'Would you please call Kermit to the phone, then, Mr. Cox, for it is to him I wish to speak.' Mr. Cox replied, however, that he had no intention of doing so, for Kermit was in the throes of nearly complete collapse. 'The throes of collapse?' I inquired, acting surprised, though, of course, I was not . . ."

"Of course you were not!" Madame Girard nodded.

"Throes?" Malcolm wondered, frowning.

" 'The little man cannot under any circumstances speak to you, Girard Girard,' Mr. Cox then said."

" 'But I am asking you,' I said to Mr. Cox, 'humbly. We are

ready to go to our country house, and it is imperative that he go with us, or Malcolm cannot accompany us either. Three people are waiting for his answer.' "

" 'The answer,' Mr. Cox then told me, 'is NO.' "

"No!" Malcolm cried, pounding his head with his fist.

" '*No* for how long, Mr. Cox?' I then asked him," Girard Girard said.

" '*No* forever,' Mr. Cox replied."

"Forever," Malcolm said.

"And he refused to allow a man of your caliber to talk with Kermit." Madame Girard was pale with indignation.

"Mr. Cox told me that Kermit would never be able to say yes again to anything." Girard Girard finally brought out the statement.

"No!" Malcolm cried, but Madame Girard raised her hand for silence.

" 'And do not call Kermit again,' Mr. Cox commanded me," Girard Girard went on. " 'I will call *you* should he ever say yes in the interim.' "

"Then why in hell did you look so merry when you came back here to the car?" Madame Girard demanded to know of her husband.

"I was only laughing at Mr. Cox's tyranny," Girard Girard said. "He is a prig, too, as well as a tyrant."

"A prig?" Malcolm paused over the word.

"Oh, that always goes with tyranny!" Madame Girard tossed aside Malcolm's confusion.

"To think I had almost entrusted my life to Mr. Cox," Malcolm said, almost whispering.

"So you had." Girard Girard was firm about this.

"And now he has such power over Kermit!" Malcolm remarked.

"He can't do anything to Kermit." Madame Girard was positive.

"Because he is a prig or a tyrant?" Malcolm wondered.

"What has his prighood to do with his power?" Madame Girard inquired. "His prighood is only his manner. Mr. Cox's power emanates from another source. But on Kermit it is wasted."

"I see," Malcolm said.

"He will never win," Girard Girard said.

"Never," Madame Girard agreed.

They all three sat there thinking of how Mr. Cox, however, did have Kermit, and the wires were, so to speak, down, or at least in the hands only of Mr. Cox.

Then Girard started the motor.

"Where are you taking us?" Madame Girard exclaimed.

"For a drive about the water."

"But not to the country estate!" Malcolm warned.

"Oh, do you think we could go after this shattering experience?" Madame Girard scoffed. "Not even if I had a whole cave of dark rum waiting for me!"

"We will go to the country tomorrow," Girard said. "My lungs must have that air!"

"We will go when I give the command, and not until," Madame Girard said, suddenly removing her veil, and as she did so, Malcolm gasped to see her beautiful, though haggard, eyes again.

"You talk of your lungs!" Madame Girard scoffed. "But you never consider my *thirst*!"

Girard Girard opened his mouth to say something.

"Silence!" Madame Girard anticipated him.

"Do you ever consider my thirst?" she vociferated again.

But again when Girard Girard attempted to reply, Madame Girard cried out first: "Do not open your mouth. Silence!"

Malcolm held his head in his hands.

"Girard Girard," Madame Girard said, shaking the veil at him, "have you ever given my thirst at any time the serious attention, say, Professor Cox has given it—the very few times he has given it? You may answer this question."

"I have," Girard Girard replied, somewhat bashfully, as Malcolm thought.

"You lie!" she screamed. "You lie in front of this innocent boy witness."

They drove on for a moment of silence.

"It's so infernal to be thirsty, and to have your thirst inter-
dicted," she said in a whisper. She wept a little, then bracing
herself, she cried: "Your lungs can rot! Do you hear? Rot!"

Address No. 4

~~~~~~

"Yes, it's *you,*" Mr. Cox said, without any real surprise, but with a sourer tone than Malcolm had ever heard in the astrologer's voice before. "While everybody thinks you are living in Madame Girard's country house, here you are on the bench—as if nothing had happened to you since your father's death."

"I couldn't go to the country without Kermit," Malcolm said, no conviction in his expression. "The Girards were too . . . *imposing*"—here Malcolm borrowed a word—"too imposing to be alone with."

"Subterfuges! Dodges! Oh, how I know you." Mr. Cox shook his head. Today he carried a fancy toothpick in his mouth, and his tone seemed even more cutting and insolent than usual.

"Everyone in and out of the Girards' spoke slightingly of you," Malcolm told Mr. Cox, with the expression of one merely vacantly reporting the facts.

"Those in the possession of the truth are hardly ever thought well of," Mr. Cox said coolly enough.

"You are in the . . . possession . . . of . . . ?" and Malcolm stood up briefly, but sat down just as quickly at a gesture from his mentor.

"I thought you knew I had it," Mr. Cox said calmly, a little pleasant humor coming into his face.

"I don't believe I would *care* to have it," Malcolm said finally, a bit disconsolate again.

"Well, dear boy." Mr. Cox considered this. "I think you have accomplished a great deal without it. That sometimes happens, you know. But in your case, too, you don't need to worry about it—because you're not going to be bothered with having it!"

"I suppose when you say I've accomplished a great deal—you mean my conquest of Madame and Mr. Girard," Malcolm said.

"Who else?" The astrologer nodded.

"Madame Girard relies on you an awful lot, too," Malcolm thought aloud. "Yet she continually condemns you, as does Girard Girard."

Mr. Cox removed his toothpick from his mouth, but did not reply.

"You are a magician, as they say—as well as an astrologer," and Malcolm shook his head at the complexity of things.

Mr. Cox did not bother to reply to this statement, but hurried on:

"All the people whom I stir to action—and there are an awful lot of them, let me tell you—they *somehow* fail . . ."

"But what are the actions you stir them to?" Malcolm complained because he did not, as usual, understand.

"Mind you," Mr. Cox went on, "I don't care how much they talk against me, or how much they talk with one another—though the only real talking *I* will do. But I want them to act out the parts they are meant to act out with one another!"

"And what parts would those ever be?" Malcolm wondered, not able at that moment to smother a wide yawn.

Mr. Cox waited for Malcolm to close his mouth.

"I have arranged all the situations." Mr. Cox spoke without his usual optimism. "Why can't *they* act? I have brought the right people together, and the right situations. I'm not such a fool as not to know *right people* and *right situations* when they're together. But nothing happens. Nothing at all."

"You *may* have made a mistake!" Malcolm boldly suggested.

"No, no, Malcolm," and the astrologer was quite gentle now. "It's the stars." Mr. Cox spoke with resignation in his voice. "What else can you call it? There's just no help for it. Everything is played out."

"You mean I've left the bench, then, for no reason at all?"

"No, Malcolm, we won't give up, stars or no, though I may have to pay for this remark later," and Mr. Cox whistled in a simulation of high spirits. "For if the Girards didn't win over the forces"—here the astrologer looked furtively to the horizon —"perhaps this might do the trick, as a desperate remedy"— and he pulled out a small card and thrust it into the hand of his young friend.

"Another address!" Malcolm crowed.

"Do your rejoicing later." Mr. Cox was again severe. "And as to enthusiasm, child, get rid of it. It can only lead you to commitments, and not just *some,* but a legion. Fear it . . . Now, go to it, and we may meet again, and if not, well, then not, and may success be yours."

Taking out his toothpick from his mouth, and giving Malcolm a vigorous farewell nod, Mr. Cox left just as unceremoniously and quickly as ever.

"You're the new boy?" Eloisa Brace said, looking out at Malcolm from the basement door of her three-story house, but not opening the door to him.

Malcolm was listening to the sound of the alto sax which was coming from upstairs, but his glimpse of the strong chin and fierce blue eyes of Eloisa Brace stopped him a little. He had never seen such a strong-looking woman. He couldn't tell her age because she looked so imposing. Her blond hair was long and thick and hid her forehead.

"Malcolm?" Eloisa Brace inquired. "Is it you?"

He nodded.

"O.K., then, either come in or go out. You can't just stand

there, O.K., you know. I'm giving a concert."

Eloisa Brace said a few more O.K.'s, for she put this expression after every few words she uttered.

"Mr. Cox . . ." Malcolm began.

"Yes, yes, O.K.," Eloisa Brace told him, irritability and impatience rising anew in her.

"You're awfully *cross* tonight, aren't you?" Malcolm asked her.

Eloisa opened the basement door at last, and Malcolm went partially inside the room.

"Is that the new boy?" a man's voice demanded, and a young man with a beard and thick glasses hurried down the back staircase which led from the concert room above to the basement where Malcolm and Eloisa were now standing.

"Will you please take over from here, O.K." Eloisa Brace turned to the young man. "You know I can't stand kids. And the musicians are waiting."

Eloisa let out a great sigh of relief and disappeared up the stairs which the young bearded man had just descended.

"My wife is a bit nervous when we have the concerts," he told Malcolm.

"Eloisa Brace is *your* wife?" Malcolm asked.

The young man nodded. "But do come clear into the room, why don't you? Don't stand against the door," he asked Malcolm.

Malcolm came further into the room, and became immediately absorbed in looking at the furnishings about him: it was not unlike Estel Blanc's—only, if anything, gloomier, but as at Estel's, paintings adorned all the walls, but here there was a great display of stuffed birds, especially owls sitting on varnished perches, and the furniture was all very old and worn, like what one would expect on a farm.

"Yes," the young man told Malcolm, "you are just as Mr. Cox described you," and he held his spectacles against his eyes to see the boy more clearly.

The man was very friendly, though rather in the manner of a doctor, and Malcolm smiled under this attention. He thought that this man was perhaps the most friendly person he had ever met.

"Some wine, Malcolm?" The man handed him a cracked jelly-glass filled with red liquor.

"I usually don't drink," Malcolm replied.

"Do have some," his new friend urged him.

"You're so . . . very polite," the boy noted.

"You're much nicer than I even thought you would be for a boy of your class," the man said. "My name, by the way, is Jerome."

Malcolm accepted Jerome's hand, and smiled.

"I don't suppose you have heard of me," Jerome inquired, a vague hopeful emotion coming into his voice.

"Just as the husband of Eloisa Brace," Malcolm told him.

"Well, of course, Eloisa is at present a bit more famous than me," Jerome admitted. "As a painter, you understand." He pointed to the paintings on the wall, which were by Eloisa.

Malcolm looked at the paintings now again. They were portrayals of a woman wandering at night, a woman with long hair and a strong chin, but with a soft, kind, even moony expression, garbed in a long flowing robe. The different women depicted in the paintings, Malcolm decided, both were and were not Eloisa. The real Eloisa was so much crosser and older in everyday life.

"Didn't Mr. Cox tell you what I was famous for?" Jerome brought Malcolm's attention back from the paintings to himself.

"No," Malcolm replied. "He just mentioned you as Eloisa's husband."

"How typical of Mr. Cox," Jerome said.

Then: "You see," Jerome went on, "I was in prison."

"I see." Malcolm tasted his wine, and nodded.

"For burglary," Jerome informed him.

"How did you ever come to get here, then?" Malcolm wondered, and he pointed to the room in which they were now sitting.

"You charming fellow," Jerome laughed. He poured Malcolm some more wine. "I've heard all about you and your *bench*!"

"But—" Malcolm began by way of explanation, and surprise.

"No more need be said, sir," Jerome cried, raising the palm of his hand. "It's all all right here. Everything is all right here."

"But you said you were a burglar," Malcolm managed to get out.

Jerome tasted his wine with loud deliberative smacks. "That's right," he finally said. "I got ten years for it. The state pen."

"You must have . . . stolen an awful lot," Malcolm decided.

Jerome laughed. "Somehow *you* can say that," he told Malcolm. "Yes, Malcolm, I stole one hell of a lot."

At that moment Jerome seemed to have forgotten all about Malcolm, and he merely looked out past where they were sitting into the inner darkness of the next room. Then coming back to his guest, Jerome said, "Yes, Malcolm, you are looking at nothing less than an ex-con."

"I'm very proud to know you," Malcolm said, and he finished his second glass.

"Do you know what I am talking about, Malcolm?" Jerome said more gravely, but still with great friendliness.

"Yes," Malcolm said thoughtfully. "I was just wondering, though, if Estel Blanc may perhaps have at one time—maybe not for ten years, you know—*been* one."

"Estel Blanc!" Jerome's smile faded into an offended and shocked look. "Why, he's not in our class at all! For one thing, he's a total snob. Whatever made you think he would be an ex-con."

But Malcolm's sunny calm restored Jerome's good humor.

Malcolm, however, continued: "You see," he said, "I don't really know what an ex-con should look like on account of you seem just like anybody nice to me."

"Like anybody nice?" Jerome smiled.

"Well, maybe not so awfully impressively nice as Girard Girard, say," Malcolm reconsidered. "But in so many ways you are so much sweeter than he is."

"*Sweet*—O.K., thank you, Malcolm," Jerome said, and he was at that moment, anybody could see, very sweet, and he smiled, perhaps thinking of his own sweetness.

"You and I, Malcolm, are quite different in all things—in every way—and yet we like one another, and we are alike," Jerome told him. "Here," he pointed out, "you're not drinking up."

He poured Malcolm some more wine.

"But you see—I don't drink," Malcolm reminded him.

Jerome made the tasting sounds again from his own replenished glass.

"Jerome—what *is* an ex-con?" Malcolm said suddenly.

Jerome stopped tasting. He paused. "A man who's been in prison. An ex-convict, you know," he replied without looking at the boy.

"And you really *were* in prison." Malcolm considered this.

"Here," Jerome pointed out to him, "I wrote a book about it."

"How difficult *that* must have been," Malcolm observed.

"Would you like to read my book?" Jerome inquired, eagerness and anticipation in his expression.

Malcolm was about to tell Jerome that he could not say, for he had never read a *complete* book, when Jerome, without waiting for an answer, hastened to a little closet nearby where there was piled a stack of books, all with the same title, and brought one copy back to Malcolm.

The book's title was *They Could Have Me Back.*

"What a nice title," Malcolm said. "Is that you naked on the cover?"

Jerome smiled and touched Malcolm lightly on the ear.

From upstairs came the thick rich tones of the sax and the bass.

"Do you dig that music, Malcolm?" Jerome kept his mouth very close to Malcolm as he said this.

Malcolm half-smiled.

"I don't read very much," Malcolm explained, handing the book back to Jerome.

Malcolm put his hand slowly to the place on his ear where Jerome had touched him.

"What was that for?" Malcolm said.

"Look, Malcolm," Jerome said, "I know you make a point of being dumb, but you're not that dumb."

Just then the music upstairs stopped, and Jerome hastened away from Malcolm and sat down on the floor and began talking very fast about how he was a writer and was now finishing a study of delinquency among minors.

Footsteps sounded on the staircase.

"Jerome, are you coming up here or not?" Eloisa Brace's voice sounded severe, but shaky.

"In a minute, darling," Jerome said.

"Look," she continued, "the musicians want to see you about the arrangement for the new number. Please consider others for once in your life. Is that boy still down there?"

When there was no answer either from Jerome or Malcolm, Eloisa cried: "Don't keep me waiting now, after all my trouble to bring Grig and Goody together here tonight," and they heard her footsteps retreating upstairs.

"My wife." Jerome smiled both sweetly and sadly, and he winked at Malcolm.

Malcolm looked down at his empty glass.

"More?" Jerome said.

Malcolm made no effort to refuse, and Jerome poured another brimming glass.

"I do want you to read my book," Jerome said, sitting on the floor by Malcolm's chair now, and grasping the boy's foot lightly. "I want you to because, well, because I guess you don't seem to have any prejudgments about anything. Your eyes are completely open."

Jerome pulled on Malcolm's pant cuff.

"Look, Malcolm," he said suddenly, "I'm not a queer or anything, so don't jump like that when I touch you. You do something to me because I guess you just seem like the spirit of . . . life, or something, and I wouldn't have said anything so corny before in all my life. But hell, you do."

"I see," Malcolm said, and he looked down at Jerome's hand which rested on his leg.

"Will you be a good friend, then?" Jerome asked Malcolm.

"Of course, Jerome," Malcolm cried, like one startled from sleep.

"Thank you, Malcolm."

They sat now close together, while upstairs the music had begun again.

"It's going to be a wonderful friendship," Jerome said thickly, his mouth pressed against Malcolm's trouser legs. "But you must give up Mr. Cox and Girard Girard. They won't do for you at all. They don't believe in what you and I believe in . . ."

"But what do we believe in?" Malcolm said, and he made a motion to stand up.

"Sit still." Jerome put his hand on the boy's knee with force. "Just sit still, please."

Jerome cocked his head, swallowing the wine in his glass.

"What do we believe in, Malcolm? What a pleasant, pleasant question. I'm so awfully glad you said *we*. I will appreciate that a long time. A hell of a long time from now I will think of that question of yours, Malcolm: what do WE believe in. You carry me right back to something, Malc . . ."

"You see, I don't know what I be—"

"Don't spoil it, Malc. Don't say another word."

"Jerome." Malcolm's voice came shaky and tiny now.

"Don't spoil anything now!" Jerome commanded again, his eyes soft and half-closed. "Don't speak."

At that moment, the glass fell out of Malcolm's hand, and without another syllable, the boy toppled unconscious out of his chair and onto Jerome's lap, head first.

"Jesus Christ," Jerome said, opening his eyes.

A portrait is begun

~~~~~~

Malcolm woke up in a very small bed unlike his own, without a canopy, and found himself with a wall against him on one side and on the other a dark-skinned man who was snoring.

Malcolm had never, he thought, since the probable death of his father, seen such a distinguished-looking man.

Still somewhat asleep, the boy said, "Are you by chance, then, royalty, sir?" It was a kind of rhetorical question, an echo from Madame Girard's rather than anything that Malcolm meant to address to his bedfellow. But the dark-skinned man frowned, and quit snoring.

"Sir." Malcolm pushed the man, addressing him now directly. "Who are you?"

When there was no answer, Malcolm looked about him. There was no way to get out of bed without practically pushing the dark man out of bed at the same time, for the bed was much too small for two persons—it was too small for the majestic type of person who was sleeping next to him, and Malcolm, already pinioned against the wall side of the bed, could not move without pushing the stranger.

At that moment, the man opened one eye, then the other, and then yawned widely.

"Sir," Malcolm began again, "this is the first time I have not slept in my own bed, and I am quite surprised."

The dark man nodded, still yawning from time to time, and then scratched slowly and deeply under his armpits.

"Who are you, sir?" Malcolm inquired again.

"I know who you are," the man replied, and he looked pleasant and calm, though grave.

"You have an even richer voice than Estel Blanc," Malcolm noted, but was about to correct himself at once for having mentioned the unpopular undertaker, and there was, furthermore, no connection between the two, he realized, except that, of course, they were both of the Abyssinian race.

The man reached behind their common pillow and brought out a handsome small comb with which he began tidying his hair and beard, while excusing himself for doing so.

"I don't suppose you *are* . . . royalty, though please forgive me if you are," Malcolm said.

"Well, forgive *me*—for forgetting to introduce myself, Malcolm. George Leeds, sir, the piano player with the quartet."

Malcolm shook hands with George Leeds and told him how pleased he was to meet him.

"Everybody who is a friend of mine calls me Grig," George Leeds then added.

"May I see your hands, then, Grig?" Malcolm asked.

"Oh, I'm not lying to you about my profession." George Leeds smiled, stretching out his hands for Malcolm's inspection.

"Those are piano player hands," Malcolm commented.

"Well, I'm not royalty, kiddo," George told him. "Not the royalty you're talking about."

"May I borrow your comb now, sir?" Malcolm inquired, and George passed it to him with a short bow.

"So you passed out in the basement last night," George Leeds commented.

"Passed out?" Malcolm frowned, wondering, and putting down the comb briefly.

George Leeds stared at him, and then speaking slow, pronouncing each syllable as to a foreigner: "DRUNK. FELL UN-CON-SCIOUS. At feet of your host."

"Jerome the burglar!" Malcolm remembered, with a short snort of recognition.

George Leeds smiled, and stretching out hugely, cracked the bones in his spine.

"That seems a hundred years ago," Malcolm said, passing the comb back to George.

"Jerome a hundred years ago?" George inquired.

"My father seems a thousand years ago," Malcolm told him.

"By the way, what's the slant on this father of yours? Seems that's all people talk about in this part of town: is he or ain't he, et cetera."

"Oh, he's been dead or disappeared for nearly a year now," Malcolm said. "Mr. Cox has been introducing me to all of his address people, you see, and that is how I got in with Jerome."

"Got in with him?" George turned about painfully in the narrow space of the bed, and took a better look at the boy.

"Nearly every day, you see, Mr. Leeds, I get a different address. I'm beginning life, I guess you might call it. You would never believe all the people I get to meet," Malcolm explained, but so close were the confines of their sleeping quarters, he found himself speaking directly into the piano player's ear, as one would to a stone-deaf person.

"I think maybe I do believe it," George Leeds replied, and then he put his hand on Malcolm's forehead. "No," he said, after a pause, "you don't have no fever."

"Thank you," Malcolm said, immediately putting his hand to where George Leeds had placed his.

Malcolm was just about to tell George Leeds about Kermit and the Girards when Eloisa Brace entered the room bearing a tray of steaming coffee.

"O.K., how are all of my *fellows* this morning," Eloisa said. There was no trace of her irritability of the night before.

She kissed both of them briefly on the forehead, and handed each of them his cup of coffee.

"Cramped quarters." Eloisa commented on the bed.

"This is his first night in a strange bed," George Leeds pointed out to Eloisa Brace, cocking his head at Malcolm.

"I slept very well," Malcolm replied ceremoniously.

"Fine, fine," Eloisa said.

"And I think I know the reason why," Malcolm continued.

Eloisa and George stared at him.

"It's because the piano player smells like coconuts," Malcolm said with a kind of slow triumph.

'Coconuts!" George Leeds exclaimed. "I accept that as a compliment, Malcolm."

Malcolm was about to continue speaking when Eloisa Brace said that she wanted a word with him alone as soon as possible.

"I hope it's not about anything personal and serious." Malcolm was disturbed.

"It is and it isn't," Eloisa told him. "The fact is," she said, and she began tidying up the bottom of the bedclothes a bit, "I would like to paint you, Malcolm."

Malcolm smiled insipidly.

"Eloisa wants to draw your *portrait*," the piano player further explained to the boy.

Malcolm nodded.

"Good," Eloisa Brace said. "It's a commissioned portrait, practically, you see," she went on. "I have an idea Madame Girard may want it, once it is completed. So we must begin immediately after you've had your coffee . . ."

"But I have to go to the bench some time this morning," Malcolm explained.

"Bench?" Eloisa said, for she had only vaguely heard of this aspect of Malcolm's life. "No, no, we've made all the arrangements with your hotel manager. You're to move in here while you're having your portrait done."

"With the piano player?" Malcolm stared at George Leeds.

"Well, not exactly. You will, I mean, have a room *somewhere*, though my house is just full up at the moment. O.K.? Well, hurry, Malcolm," Eloisa Brace commanded. "We don't have too much time to lose."

"Is this all correct?" Malcolm turned to the piano player.

Yawning, George Leeds replied: "You see, Malcolm, I just

stick to the piano. And the rest of the world and the people, too, even nice people like you, well, I just kind of tend to let them go, if you don't mind me saying so."

Eloisa Brace watched Malcolm, waiting.

"Eloisa has already begun his portrait!" Mr. Cox was speaking to Kermit, who was lying on the sofa in his own studio, covered in quilts, sick with a bad cold.

"Everywhere Malcolm goes, flowers spring up," Kermit commented hoarsely.

Mr. Cox paused lengthily, then said: "He was simply lucky enough to have found us."

"You mean, of course"—Kermit sat bolt upright in the sofa—"lucky enough to have met you." His nostrils palpitated from his exertion.

"Let's not quarrel when you're ill," Mr. Cox said.

"Quarreling is something nobody can forbid me," Kermit reminded him. "When I cease to quarrel, I will cease to be."

Mr. Cox was about to make some comment, perhaps metaphysical, on this remark, when Kermit hurried ahead of him:

"I can hardly wait, nonetheless, to see Eloisa Brace's portrait of Malcolm."

"But your sharp little eyes can surely visualize it already," Mr. Cox rejoined.

"No, my sharp *little* eyes cannot!" Kermit sat up all the way now on the divan, and put his feet on the floor, and with a loud bang put on his derby hat, which he usually wore only when he was painting.

"All of Eloisa's portraits, whether they are of her or others, look just like Eloisa," Mr. Cox reminded him.

"This one will be different." Kermit was emphatic.

"You seem to be praising another artist," Mr. Cox cautioned, "—which, I must say, is a new tack for you to take."

"Did I say anything in praise of Eloisa Brace? I wouldn't dream of doing that. She can't paint, and she can't draw, and she can't even see. But"—and here Kermit threw off the covers of his bed onto the floor, and stood up solidly—"she does have a definite feeling for young men like Malcolm, and that feeling will triumph in this case and produce a good painting, perhaps a masterpiece. That often happens to painters without talent—they do one fine thing."

"All you're saying is you're a bit partial to Malcolm." Mr. Cox shook his head.

"All I can say is I live only to see that finished portrait," Kermit replied.

"The thought that Malcolm is living there is more interesting to me than that he is being painted," Mr. Cox pointed out.

"It must be a good deal more strenuous than living in a whorehouse," Kermit observed. "I suppose the poor boy has already been taken to bed by a score of people there."

"Eloisa did speak to me a bit—almost on that very subject," Mr. Cox began. "She is sorry, she told me, that Malcolm cannot have a room of his own as he did in his hotel. And she runs such a busy house, you know—all those traveling musicians coming and going at all hours—that Malcolm has to sleep with a different person each night, and sometimes, when there is real crowding, Eloisa has to move him in the middle of the night to a different bed. Often it's more apt to be three in a bed than two . . . Malcolm told Eloisa that it was like traveling in Czechoslovakia during a war."

"I'm glad for his own sake that Malcolm's father is dead," Kermit said, and he pulled his derby hat low over his eyes.

"There you go again, with your lower-middle-class prejudices coming out," Mr. Cox exploded. "Everybody has to begin sometime, and Malcolm is beginning."

Kermit shook his head. Then: "What will Eloisa Brace do with the portrait?" Kermit asked.

"But I thought you knew." Mr. Cox pooh-poohed his pretension of ignorance.

"What could I know, lying here in my widowerhood?" Kermit demanded to know, and he walked over to his easel, where an empty canvas stared at him. He put a few strokes on it with a pencil, and then put the pencil down.

"Everybody knows Eloisa will sell the portrait to Madame Girard," Mr. Cox said.

Kermit nodded, a slow strange smile on his mouth.

"Oh, to be wanted, adored, sought after," Kermit began, and he went back to his bed, took up a small bottle of camphor, and smelled of it. "A boy comes in off a summer bench," the midget continued, "and is immediately wined, dined, courted, carried off in private limousines, *painted,* while I, with all my talents and training and charm—well, Mr. Cox, it's the ashcan for me, that's about all anyone can honestly say."

Mr. Cox got up to leave, humming. "You had your chance, I'm afraid," the astrologer said gravely.

"Before you go," Kermit said in a low voice, his eyes looking away from Mr. Cox, "answer me one simple question: Does Malcolm have any mind at all?"

"I will answer your question with another one: Do you think he needs one?" Mr. Cox said, and he was already at the door which led to the street, which he opened, without another word of parting to the midget.

"I can't help being interested in jazz musicians any more than a fish can keep out of water," Eloisa Brace confessed, as she was painting Malcolm's portrait. "Jazz musicians are my fare, and almost always have been."

"Doesn't Jerome interfere?" Malcolm wondered.

"Move your chin just a little more to the right, hon," Eloisa told him.

Returning to his question, she smiled, then said: "Jerome knew everything about me when he married me. We both knew the chances we were taking."

Malcolm nodded, but kept his chin in place.

"I gave up a rich husband for Jerome." She stopped painting, perhaps remembering briefly that earlier marriage and husband. "But I've never regretted it. Not that we're happy, Jerome and I. We've never known a day of rest. While with my first husband, I was *outwardly* happy, you see—had nothing but rest. But with Jerome, well, I don't have a thing, and not really a happy moment. Get poorer every day—he can't find work because of what he is, and we do nothing but quarrel. But, Malcolm, it's *life* with Jerome . . . Here I am, telling you everything," she said, squinting at the portrait, for she was more than a little nearsighted.

"But when do you find time to be married?" Malcolm asked, and added, at the look he got from Eloisa: "I mean with so many jazz concerts going on and all."

"Marriage is something that just goes on and on inside of you, Malcolm," Eloisa said. "Concerts begin and end, and musicians come and go, but a real marriage just keeps going."

She painted slowly and rhythmically now, a soft look on her mouth.

Malcolm cleared his throat vociferously.

"It was Jerome, you see, I was worried about," the boy finally said.

"Jerome?" Eloisa wondered, putting her brush down, and taking up a second, smaller one in its place. "Why on earth should anybody worry about Jerome?" She frowned. "For the first time in his whole life he's *safe*."

"Well, it's so sad he has to remember he's an ex-con all the time," Malcolm noted.

"Oh, everybody's entitled to a few memories when he's potted." Eloisa shrugged this off. "And marriage has taken the place of all that old prison trouble. He just likes to remember when he's potted is all. Grown-up people, you see, Malcolm, have long memories: you remember that."

"Poor, poor Jerome," Malcolm exclaimed softly.

Just then the telephone rang. Eloisa sat still, looking gloomy and thoughtful, and then turning to Malcolm, she inquired: "Would you have the heart to answer that, and then come and tell me who it is? But don't tell whoever it is that I am in."

Malcolm nodded, and going over to the little stand where the telephone rested, took off its receiver.

He paused, listening to the cascade of sounds at the other end of the wire; then, looking up at Eloisa with wide eyes, he whispered: "Just guess. It's Madame Girard!"

Eloisa raised her eyes to the ceiling.

"Will you talk?" Malcolm asked Eloisa.

"I don't suppose I have any choice in the matter," the painter said. And she took the receiver from Malcolm's hands.

"I know you are lonely, my dear," Eloisa said to Madame Girard on the phone. "But you can't *can't* come here. No, no, no, my dear, you cannot!"

"But you have a young man there named Malcolm," Madame Girard's voice boomed. "And I wish to bring him to my home to stay. No, I haven't as yet considered adoption. It's not quite that kind of relationship, but of course it may come to that."

"But, Madame Girard," Eloisa implored. "You know I am painting his portrait." Eloisa regretted she had given this piece of information at once.

"Then I must purchase it at once," Madame Girard exclaimed. "Do you hear . . . I have not been so taken with a young person in years."

Eloisa motioned to Malcolm to fetch her the tray with the brandy decanter and glass, which he brought to her in a trice.

"What are those oral sounds I am now hearing?" Madame Girard asked a moment later.

"I'm sipping brandy," Eloisa explained to her.

"At nine-thirty in the morning?" Madame Girard interrogated suspiciously.

"Telephones always upset me so, Madame Girard, you know that, and when it's a long phone conversation, often a finger of brandy gets me through."

"I know *nothing* of your habits," Madame Girard replied. "All I know is Malcolm is there, when he should be here, and I must come for him. I discovered him, and I claim him."

"Madame Girard, listen to reason!"

"Why should you people who have no money or background be entrusted with him?" Madame Girard said. "Let those who can, take him."

"But the portrait," Eloisa cried. "You forget that I am doing his portrait—which you say you one day will purchase."

"You can come to the Château and finish it," Madame Girard told her.

"I cannot, and I will not, Madame Girard." Eloisa stood firm.

"I am claiming my own is all," Madame Girard said, more calm now. "I am simply asking you to hand over Malcolm. He's no longer on his bench, and I have as good a claim as anyone. We want him to go to the country, and I need his special kind of companionship. Girard Girard, as you know, is no comfort to me any more. I need youth and freshness around me. I am imploring you, Eloisa."

"Think of the brandy I am having to consume, Madame Girard, to sustain me in this telephone conversation," Eloisa appealed.

"Eloisa, I will have Girard Girard send a whole case up to you for your unpleasant task. What brand did you say you use?"

"Oh, please, you know we buy only a cheap domestic."

"You shall be sent *Napoleon* today," Madame Girard assured her.

"No favors, please." Eloisa rejected her. "You know what Jerome thinks of favors. And Malcolm must absolutely stay until the portrait is done."

"No, no, you shall come here to paint him. Meanwhile, I am getting ready to make my visit to you at once."

"We will bar the door, Madame Girard. Your wealth and position cannot force open the entry to a private house."

"You are rejecting my friendship and my generosity," Madame Girard cried. "You are rejecting *me.* When all I wish to do is *give.* Why, why cannot *you* see reason?"

"Malcolm is not going to be handed over to you. When his portrait is finished, we will call you up—not until."

"You wish, I see, then, for me to employ force," Madame Girard said with regret.

"Consider me. Consider Malcolm," Eloisa now implored her.

"Consider you. Consider him." Madame Girard harumphed. "You poor innocent thing. What do you know of real suffering? What if your husband was in a different woman's bed each evening, and then upon his arriving home at last had time only for a business talk on the transatlantic cables. Contemplate that for suffering."

"I know, Madame Girard, your marriage is a difficult one, but consider—"

"Consider you! You have your jazz musicians. You have a loving, though idiotic, husband. You have your art. Now you have Malcolm. I have nothing."

"Madame Girard, this phone is simply weighting me down, and as a result I am drinking too much. I am not a heavy drinker like you, and as you know my brands are not imported. I won't be able to paint unless you hang up, and then you will have no portrait."

"Unless you give me permission to at least come to your home, I vow I will kill myself," Madame Girard informed her.

"Madame Girard," Eloisa said, "suicide is your own decision. I will not respond to your customary threats."

"Eloisa," Madame Girard cried. "Be generous, if you cannot be reasonable. I will pay you . . . anything."

Eloisa suddenly hung up, without replying.

"She may kill herself this time," Eloisa said, taking a drink of brandy. "But I rather fear we will see her instead as a visitor here."

Malcolm nodded gravely.

"But whatever happens in these next few days or hours, or even weeks," Eloisa said, going over to Malcolm, and straightening his necktie, "don't leave, do you hear? No matter what happens. Don't go away with anybody. Your portrait must be finished, do you hear?"

Madame Girard confronts Eloisa

At that moment, George Leeds, the piano player, appeared in the room in evening dress and announced to Eloisa that the concert was about to begin on the third floor and that her presence was seriously "in request."

Malcolm was about to say something to George—how different he looked from the man who had combed his hair in their common bed!—who nodded affably at the boy, but Eloisa began giving Malcolm instructions before regretfully excusing herself, and warning him not to leave the room under any circumstances, and that she would return just as soon as the concert ended.

Eloisa and the piano player then went out together, and a few minutes later, the sad persistent notes of bass and sax, piano and vibraphone and drums drifted down to him.

Malcolm felt himself then entirely alone, more alone than had he remained on the bench. In the lonely emptiness of the house, with its castlelike high ceilings, the feel of the gray thick carpets beneath his feet, and the self-portraits of Eloisa, the drawings of Negroes looking out from their pale eyes, of strange perhaps nonexistent animals gazing at him from canvases everywhere, Malcolm remembered his early travels with his father in countries whose names he could no longer recall. But this time, he was more hopelessly alone, in addition to not understanding anything around him. And at the same time he rather felt that perhaps he belonged here as much as anywhere, with the colored musicians, the paintings, and the different bed each night.

A cat came up from the basement and examined him with a look, and then went on to the floor above. The three floors in the house were all of them furnished with identical furniture and with Eloisa's paintings, and all of them punctuated hour by hour with the notes from the bass and sax and piano.

Everywhere in the house, no matter at what hour, one felt that it was afternoon, late afternoon breaking into twilight, with a coolness, too, like perpetual autumn, an autumn that will not pass into winter owing to some damage perhaps to the machinery of the cosmos. It will go on being autumn, go on being cool, but slowly, slowly everything will begin to fall piece by piece, the walls will slip down ever so little, the strange pictures will warp, the mythological animals will move their eyes slightly for the last time as they fade into indistinction, the strings of the bass will loosen and fall, the piano keys wrinkle and disappear into the wood of the instrument, and the beautiful alto sax shrivel into foil.

How long Malcolm slept he did not know, but waking up suddenly he first saw the cat looking at him again, and then— Kermit.

"The little man," Malcolm exclaimed. "You've escaped!"

Kermit laughed, a mischievous curl of pleasure on his lips. "I was about to turn you into a cat," he told Malcolm.

"Be seated at once," Malcolm commanded, like a man in his own house. "How did you come to get in here?"

"The door was open, and I walked in from my morning stroll," Kermit informed him.

"I didn't know you ever took . . . strolls," Malcolm said with some surprise. "You're not *afraid*?"

"Afraid a dog will swallow me?" Kermit laughed, an edge of bitterness in his expression.

"I'm afraid for you . . . is all." Malcolm was serious.

"And so the great woman painter and jazz queen has succeeded in making you a prisoner," Kermit began.

"She may have," Malcolm acknowledged, "but then perhaps I was one before."

"I see you as one, yes," Kermit agreed. "But, from the bench . . . to the cathouse, which I suppose one could call it. Well . . ."

Kermit laughed somewhat too heartily, while Malcolm merely sat with his hands in his lap.

"I am, you see, *persona non grata* here," Kermit said when he had finished laughing, "or in plain words, Eloisa hates me. It took not a little courage to come in here."

"Why does such a successful woman hate *you?*" Malcolm wondered, his chin loose, and his eyes full of puzzlement.

"It's an old feud," the little man replied, in evident relishment of what he was about to tell. "Years ago—two years, in fact—I called her on the telephone—her instrument of torture —and well, with four or five drinks to fortify me, I simply said to her, 'Eloisa, my dear, why is it I'm not good enough to ever be invited to one of your *soirées?*' She was struck speechless with whatever emotion an old retired whore like her is struck speechless with. Then while she was pinioned in her own silence, I went on: 'Is it the quality of my painting, which critics find so infinitely superior to yours, which keeps me off your list, or is it the fact that my good looks and graceful presence make your unappetizing grossness and overblown charms so especially *détestable?*' "

"You said *that?*" Malcolm leaned closer.

"I said I was drunk," Kermit replied acidly—and then going on, with all his former delight: 'She actually apologized then and there, said my not having been invited was an oversight, et cetera, and was *never* intentional, but I was not so easily appeased . . . 'There is one reason, dear Eloisa,' I went on, 'why my name was perhaps never on your list.' . . . 'What on earth reason would that be?' she cried, her voice shaking and thin . . . 'Your husband, dear Eloisa,' I told her, 'is so fond of my kisses!' "

Malcolm jumped up and walked over to a corner of the room, standing there motionless and silent like a schoolboy sent to punishment, while Kermit, laughing at his own anecdote with closed eyes, at first did not perceive his friend had walked off from him.

"What on earth are you doing in that corner?" Kermit cried, when he had recovered from his mirth. "Come out from there at once . . ."

When Malcolm did not move, Kermit went over to him, and took his hand in his.

"Has the little midget failed to entertain his royal highness?" Kermit said somewhat soberly, and he led Malcolm out from the corner.

"Sit down," the little man now commanded Malcolm, and the boy obeyed, a sober look on his face.

"Tell me, dear child," the midget said. "Are you by chance a virgin?"

Malcolm's throat moved, his vocal organs appeared to be repeating Kermit's question.

"Do I have to draw a picture for you?" The little man shot an angry glance.

"Not exactly," Malcolm replied.

"Not exactly what?" Kermit said irritably.

"Not exactly . . . a virgin, I guess," Malcolm said, and a helpless grin came over his mouth.

"Well, speak up then. God knows I'm not old enough to be your *father* . . . But if you're missing in the basic information of life, I can always take a minute out for you in the name of friendship."

Malcolm nodded.

"How many girls have you been to bed with?" the midget interrogated.

"Girls?" Malcolm swallowed.

"It's girls we are talking about," the midget proceeded.

"Well, you see, my father—" Malcolm began.

"I thought we would come to that," the midget said.

Then going up to Malcolm, and shaking the boy, the little man said: "Now see here, see here—" when the sound of heavy footsteps made both of them look up.

"Petit monstre!" Eloisa Brace cried, entering the room, and addressing Kermit. "Take your hands off Malcolm at once."

"I am caressing him, you plain fool," Kermit addressed the painter.

"Forgive me," Eloisa said quickly and contritely, perhaps recognizing the real danger of Kermit's enmity toward her. "I didn't mean to speak so sharply . . . There's been so much excitement here today."

She broke into a short sob, which she immediately controlled.

"I don't mean to not be your friend, Kermit," Eloisa continued. "Though I fear you are not mine."

"I could discuss this all so much better," Kermit explained to her, "if we had something refreshing and at the same time alcoholic to drink. Something destined perhaps for one of the many parties which I seem always to have missed here."

"Kermit, please." Eloisa's temper flashed for a minute. Then looking briefly at Malcolm, she got up, explaining that she would bring Kermit a drink at once.

"I've always heard from those who have had invitations to your parties"—Kermit detained her—"that you have excellent Spanish brandy. Do you have any today, dear Eloisa?"

Eloisa Brace covered her face with her painting hand, and sighed: "It's always this way with me. I don't have any, as a matter of fact, Kermit—not at the moment. Will you please, *please* believe me, and have something else in its stead?"

"What is in its stead?" the little man wondered, holding his index finger over his temple in the manner of one who wishes to hear an important reply.

"I have some wonderful California red wine," Eloisa cried enthusiastically, a bit too loud. "Jerome and I have just discovered it, and we can't get enough of it."

"But you did manage to keep some modicum for little visitors like me?" Kermit inquired, narrowing his eyes.

"Allow me all the hospitality I can offer you," Eloisa implored him.

"I know, dear Eloisa, that you have finer wines in your house than your California substitute—satisfying though it may be to old Jerome, who went for so many years without wine at all—"

Here Eloisa attempted to interrupt the midget with a word, but the little man clapped his hands imperiously, and continued:

"*BUT,* as *I* too am a reasonable person, and since this is my first visit to a house whose entrance has always hitherto been denied to me—I will accept, shall we say, what in serious houses is proffered to the domestics?"

"Kermit," Eloisa began, and it was only at that moment that Malcolm noticed that she was wearing an evening dress which had a rather bad tear in the behind—"Kermit, let us not spoil this afternoon. For Malcolm's sake alone. We should not let him see us as only adults should see one another!"

Kermit was preparing a reply, but Eloisa vociferated in her glad voice, "And now to your wine," and went out of the room.

"She never asked me what I wanted!" Malcolm said vacantly, like one who has only come awake.

"The idea of crashing in on us like that, without knocking or a how-do-you-do or anything. And in that ridiculous cast-off torn dress." Kermit scoffed. "And just as you were about to tell me something important, Malcolm, about yourself."

"I?" Malcolm pointed in an expression of surprise to his chest.

"Tell me at once what it was you were going to say," Kermit demanded.

Malcolm stammered, for so much, so very much had occurred, it was becoming more and more difficult to remember what had happened and when, not to mention an unimportant thing like what he was about to say a few minutes ago.

But while he was still stammering, Eloisa entered with a tray on which stood three glasses and a bottle of unlabeled red wine.

"Pardon me, Kermit, if my hands shake too much to pour you each your drink," Eloisa said. "Malcolm"—she turned to him—"would you pour each of us a drink from that bottle. O.K.?"

"First, do you have an apron for me to put on?" Malcolm inquired, looking anxiously at his suit.

Eloisa and Kermit exchanged looks.

"*I* will pour each of us whatever it is in the bottle." Kermit stepped in, a lordly contempt in his voice for both Malcolm and Eloisa.

"No, no, I will pour now," Eloisa said. "My hands have quit trembling . . ."

"But, dear Eloisa," Malcolm assured her, "I would gladly pour, but all *bartenders* wear aprons, and I was only asking—"

"Silence," Eloisa shouted. "I can't endure another thing from anyone. I will pour, do you hear?" she thundered at both of them.

And trembling, she poured in great haste three glasses full of red wine.

"To all of us!" she cried with great vigor, raising her glass.

"To Girard Girard!" Malcolm exclaimed loudly, to which he got no response from either Kermit or Eloisa Brace.

"All the time I was on the third floor attending the jazz rehearsal," Eloisa said, "I could not control my nerves. I felt—perhaps because Malcolm is here—something terrible was going to happen. I could hardly wait to get back here to see if everything was all right."

"Be happy you can lead such a full life," Kermit told Eloisa. "Accept danger as part of the risk."

"Please," Eloisa said, and she looked happy for the first time that afternoon.

"I will not *please*," Kermit told her. "You have experienced nearly everything, except perhaps being under fire in battle: marriages, musicians, art, love, all the dazzle and excitement that can only come to a figure of the arts—"

"You're rubbing it in now." Eloisa became ill-tempered again.

"No, I am speaking from the heart," Kermit assured her. "You deserve your coterie, such as it is, and you deserve your position. You have conquered where perhaps no other woman ever set foot."

"I knew it!" Eloisa cried helplessly. "You're ribbing me."

"You invented modern jazz, don't deny it." The little man went over to Eloisa's chair.

"Stop him," Eloisa implored Malcolm with a look of futility.

"And your marriage to Jerome!" Kermit went on. "Is it not the marriage of the century?"

"Kermit, stop right there with my marriage. If you go further—" and she made a frantic gesture. "I can't hear—no, not even a compliment concerning my marriage. My marriage is too close, somehow, to—"

"Too *close* to what?" a deep feminine voice cried from the entrance to the room.

All eyes looked up to see Madame Girard coming into the center of the room, a sun parasol in her hand.

Closing her eyes, and raising her parasol gently into the air, she said: "Let no one converse until I have given the sign."

Madame Girard cleared her throat, but she did not need to wait for silence: she had created the deepest kind possible.

Addressing again now her auditors, she said: "I have only come here to claim what is my own. A reasonable request. I am, of course, a reasonable woman. Let there be no interruptions, please!" Madame Girard turned to Malcolm, who had stood up only, as a matter of fact, to hear her better, but she had construed his movement as an attempt to interpolate.

"Sit down," Madame Girard commanded Malcolm *sotto voce.*

She continued, closing her eyes again:

"Why should the rest of the world know plenty, happiness, domestic satisfaction, love—while I am shut out from all these things, deprived of a woman's *human* station in life, turned in upon my own devices, and saddled"—here she opened her eyes directly and immediately upon the tray with the wine bottle, then closed them again—"*saddled* with a husband who knows not whether I am alive or dead, and cares, yes, cares—*dear* Eloisa, I can feel you are shaking your head, so stop!—cares LESS."

"Madame Girard," Eloisa managed to get out.

"Silence, I say." Madame Girard addressed herself briefly to Eloisa. "I know you are a woman of talent, perhaps genius, but your words, your advice, whatever you have to offer here this afternoon is worth no more to me than yesterday's bath water . . ."

Kermit shrank into his chair, his bravado of a moment ago completely vanished, while gazing glassily at the woman he had feared so long to meet, but who, since she kept her eyes closed, allowed him for the time being to stare at her with impunity.

Malcolm began to look sleepy, and Eloisa Brace, overcome by the day's fare of brandy, wine, fear, and confusion, began whimpering softly.

"I have been called *unreasonable* by fools," Madame Girard went on, her eyelids still tightly closed and fluttering, like a medium who sees the ghost she had never thought to catch. "I, who am the most reasonable of women, the kindest, the most generous, the one who wants to give all her love. Yes, all!"

Here, Madame Girard opened her eyes wide, and, when they fell on Eloisa, the latter cried out: "Stop her, oh, stop *her*, somebody!"

Madame Girard closed her eyes again, but then, changing her mind, she opened them suddenly and said, "Will you be quiet, lady, while I am delivering my speech? Why do you think I am here but to get you to see reason! hear reason! follow reason!"

"Reason!" Eloisa cried. "For good God's sake, why does this house not fall upon us when such words are spoken."

Kermit brought Eloisa her wine glass, which, in the confusion of Madame Girard's entrance, she had put down and left forgotten.

"I have been wronged," Madame Girard continued, and raising her parasol a bit too carelessly, caught the point of it on one of the stuffed owls which rested on the mantel, and brought it flying to the carpet, where it suddenly disintegrated into a heap of dust and feathers.

"Don't touch it," Madame Girard warned, at the signs of motion on Eloisa's part. "You shall be repaid—triple—for this damage.

"But to get back!" she went on. "*Wronged* not only by that satyr Girard Girard, who has divided his lifetime into passion for money and lust with servant girls—"

"No, no, Madame Girard, you wrong him," Malcolm exclaimed, standing up.

"Will you keep these immature ephebes seated and silent, or shall I summon someone who can?" Madame Girard turned her anger against Eloisa Brace. She was about to continue when her attention was distracted by the extreme awe written on the face of the midget.

Strolling with her parasol quickly over to where the little man sat cringing—looking, as Madame Girard later described him, like a kinkajou at noon—Madame Girard studied him closely for a moment, and then delivered a resounding kiss, as stooping, she bent over his mouth.

She immediately returned to the center of the room to resume speaking.

But Kermit, touching himself on his mouth, had exclaimed: "I have been anointed, then."

"Merely recognized, not anointed," Madame Girard informed him, aside.

"Madame Girard, my dear friend," Eloisa said, making a last effort, and rising, she took the older woman by the hand. "You must go upstairs and lie down, and I will call your husband. You are going to be very sick, if you do not listen to me now."

"Go away, my dear," Madame Girard recommended to Eloisa. "You are eternally *de trop.* I am speaking primarily to *them*—" and she pointed to the two men. "You, on the other hand, should be at work painting, supplying the world with your genius, but not appearing in public. You are too ugly to appear in public, even a public as small as this room. Let the world feast its eyes on young beauties like theirs"—and she swept her arms in the direction of Malcolm and Kermit—"but let workaday geniuses like you keep to themselves in workrooms. To your workroom, genius! To your workroom!"

"Don't you see, my dear"—Eloisa continued to hold Madame Girard by the hand—"you are bringing about a *crise*."

"Then, do *you* go to bed, my dear. I myself am fresh as a daisy. Who could not be in such company?"

"You have given me a splitting headache," Eloisa complained.

"To your workroom, then. Work is the sovereign cure for headaches. You know that. Ah, how beautiful you *were*," Madame Girard reflected softly, looking directly into Eloisa's face. "How beautiful you were before your *second* marriage. Your hair was like ripe wheat—no, don't deny that it was. A delight to the eye, and hand. And now look at it. Look at you. You have allowed that burglar to defile you, to *common* you, that's what. Even your speech is no longer dignified, harumphing O.K.'s in a stream. And you've gotten a pot on you from drinking with him. Oh, how my heart has ached for you, Eloisa. I will not deny it. But my feelings for you must not interfere with my own words of advice, which are wise and true for you: Leave this room! Go to your work! You are fit now for nothing but labor. Leave me to these beautiful young men. Did you think I came to see you? Never! Go! Leave! We have no further need of you, do we, my handsomes?"

Malcolm and Kermit both gaped at Madame Girard, too engrossed by what they heard to answer her by so much as a nod.

Eloisa began walking about the room, weeping and drinking from time to time now direct from the wine bottle.

"A woman who calls herself my friend," Eloisa said weakly.

"There is no friendship here, my dear," Madame Girard replied. "You sullied my friendship for you by marrying that jailbird. Had you cared for me you would never have gone through with such a marriage. I am here today to pay tribute to these two young men, and I implore you for the last time to leave the room. I beg, and I demand it."

"You are leaving me no choice," Eloisa Brace said with great steadiness, putting down the wine bottle.

"No choice for what?" Madame Girard asked, a hint of apprehension in her tone.

"I am going to call Girard Girard," Eloisa warned her.

"He is in Iowa making four million dollars."

"Then I shall call the authorities," Eloisa said, her voice and manner completely unlike her own.

"Authorities, your foot!" Madame Girard sneered, and she moved over to the table on which sat Malcolm's wine glass, which was more than half full, and which she now drained at a swallow. "They have called the authorities a thousand times for me," she regaled them. "But do you think they *dare* take me? When they know who I am? Never. And do you know, even if they did not *know* who I was, why they would never dare take me?" She stared at everyone in the room, all of whom, she saw, hung on each word that now came from her. "Of course you don't know why! How could you? They don't take me because I *know* everything! And they can see that knowledge on my face! For that reason, even if they should be called, they would never disturb me . . ."

Going immediately over to Malcolm after she had said this, she began kissing his sideburns, moving from one to the other in rapid succession.

"It is for you alone," Madame Girard said, "that I made this difficult trip, that I came to see your beautiful face . . . living, *and* portrayed in oil . . ."

Madame Girard stopped suddenly, like one who is listening for a sound which will be a signal and cue.

"Where is that portrait, you swindler?" She addressed Eloisa.

"Malcolm! Kermit!" Eloisa said fiercely. "We must tie her. We must tie her or she will begin to destroy things."

"*They* won't help you," Madame Girard hurled at Eloisa.

"Hold her," Eloisa commanded the boys.

Neither of the young men budged.

"You see," Madame Girard laughed. "You can do nothing. Go call your authorities."

Madame Girard had, however, forgotten one thing about Eloisa Brace: the latter's athletic prowess.

Eloisa closed her eyes, bracing herself for the supreme effort, while Madame Girard, already swaying on her feet, laughed deliriously at her imagined victory.

"I will never leave," she was crying when Eloisa Brace, looking remarkably like a boxer who has reentered the ring, advanced toward the great woman, and delivered two blows, a powerful left, and then a right to the chin, and Madame Girard tottered and then fell silently, a sad smile on her mouth, to the floor, and lay there in an attitude like that of the stone queen, asleep through all the ages.

"Pick her up and carry her to the east guest room," Eloisa commanded the two men quietly, and Malcolm and Kermit hastened to obey her.

The oration of Madame Girard

"But why should I leave your house, if you love me?" Madame
Girard was speaking to Jerome Brace, late the next day, lying
back in the largest bed in the house, to which Malcolm and
Kermit had, with great difficulty—they had dropped her twice
on the staircase—carried her.

Madame Girard held her hand to her "mouse," inflicted on
her by Eloisa, and, as Jerome noted admiringly, one of the
blackest eyes which he himself, in his own specialized career,
had ever seen.

Madame Girard was proud of Jerome's acknowledgment of
her "mouse," but soon she began to complain again of her
treatment—not so much of Eloisa's "brutality"—she had admired the painter's daring attack on her—but of Jerome's insis-
tent order that she leave the premises.

Madame Girard denied that Jerome loved her any more.

"We do love you, Madame Girard, more than you will ever
know."

"My mother used to employ that same phrase to me, and
yet it was she who ruined my life with her undiscriminating
affection."

"*I* love you, Madame Girard," Jerome said, taking her small hand in his.

"Yet you ask me to leave the premises." She shook her head.

"Only because we love you."

"Don't you realize that you are asking me to give up the one thing I now wish more than anything in the world," Madame Girard expostulated.

Jerome watched her.

"Because I am with the ones I love now," she went on. "The little Kermit—" she suddenly spoke in "baby-talk" over this phrase. "Malcolm, Eloisa, George Leeds, and the musicians, and *you,* wonderful you." She held out her arms to him, and Jerome kissed her quietly again, this time on the hair.

"It's not," Jerome began, sitting down on the bed beside her, "it's not as if you could never come to see us again."

"Oh, but it is," she replied. "It is, and you know it is."

"Madame Girard, a *little* reason, please."

"I must stay because love is here," she told him.

"You will diminish a good deal of that love if you stay!" he warned.

Her eyes darted about in her head, and then, whispering into his ear, she told him: "But I will be good—for you."

"You were never good in your life, Madame Girard. Your whole life has been devoted to not being good for your friends. And it is this quality in you that makes us love you: you cannot be good."

"I cannot?" she asked, craftiness and sweetness in her voice.

"You can NOT," Jerome repeated for her.

"But this time, I *will.* I will command myself."

"Madame Girard, consider the man you are talking to."

"Jerome, the burglar," she said, hopelessly considering her situation.

"How people of privilege always put things so coarsely," Jerome said. "It is really only the downtrodden who have all the sensitivity."

"I have suffered too much to be fine any more," she said, speaking now into the wall.

"What I was trying to tell you," Jerome continued, "is I

know men and women from prison, and I know that you don't reform by saying you mean to. Besides, you have no intention of reforming. You want to be naughty."

"I want to be?" She considered this.

"It's the only part you can play now."

"You mean I have limited myself." Madame Girard reached for one of the *brioches* which they had brought to her at her insistence.

"Consider," Jerome said, "you have acted this one part for as many years as you have been married to Girard Girard, who worships, or at least worshipped, the ground you walk on."

"Don't go into my years of marriage and my age," she warned him. "I know how old I am, and you need not give a chronicle of my life."

"I had no intention of referring to your age. But you have played your naughty role for a great long time."

"Jerome," she said, chewing the *brioche* critically, "your trouble is you have left life and gone on to religion."

He laughed, superior to this comment.

"The worst kind of change," she went on, "has happened to you. You're a reformer. A do-gooder. You think because you were a burglar and did time that you have a blueprint for everybody outside. You're every confounded preacher and evangelist I have ever known."

"Tell me what they're like."

"Like they know the answers before they even heard the question. Yes, you're one of the truth boys, and though you have a lot more honey on your tongue than most of them, *no thank you,* Jerome, *no thank you.* You've ruined Eloisa, but keep your hands off my soul."

"Madame Girard, you're being pretty hard on me."

"And don't keep addressing me with my full title," she reminded him.

"What should I call you, then?"

"Just address me with your eyes, and I'll judge you from there."

Jerome smiled, and his gaze fell down to one of Madame Girard's exposed feet, whose nails were freshly painted.

"Then there is nothing for Eloisa and me to do but what we have always done in this situation?" he said, standing up.

"Do you mean to call Girard Girard again, or only the police this time?" she wondered.

"Girard first, of course, and then, if necessary, the police."

"And to think I am talking to an ex-con," Madame Girard said. "You're as dumb and mean as any damned arm of the law you could turn to."

"We have to lead our own lives, Madame Girard," Jerome said.

"And yet you talk about love," she mused, wiping off her fingers of the crumbs from the pastry.

"By the way," she added. "That *brioche* was stale."

He bowed.

"Do you think I care, Jerome, if your *brioche* is stale? Not at all."

"Then why mention it?"

"We should mention everything. Otherwise no friendship or love is possible. You yourself have taught me that, and you are 'cured.' "

Jerome cleared his throat.

"We are not asking anything impossible of you," Jerome continued in his (as he himself could not help noticing now) *pastoral* manner. "We are merely asking you to go to your beautiful home and to your husband."

"Do you know what is happening in my beautiful home at this very moment?" Madame Girard demanded, raising her hand upward.

Jerome waited for her answer.

"Girard Girard is in bed with the laundress."

"And are you clear of any responsibility in this?"

"I suppose I am responsible for everything," she replied. "But why go home to see what my irresponsibility has produced? I ask you this, Jerome, and this time reply as your old burglar self, and not as my pastor."

"Madame Girard," Jerome began hesitatingly, and with the unmistakable note of loss of patience.

"Don't tell me you love me again, either," she warned, "or

I may lose that stale *brioche.*" She held her hand to her breast.

"I'm afraid we have no choice but to take measures with you," he said lamely, perhaps quoting something somebody had once said to him.

"Is that all?"

"Why can't you believe in us?"

"Why can't you love me enough to let me stay and enjoy my 'beauties,' Malcolm and Kermit, and my admiration for Eloisa?"

"For one thing, Malcolm is having his portrait painted, and you would upset all order and calm around here."

"I would be still as a tomb," Madame Girard begged.

"You would want to watch, you know you would. And then watching, you would begin to criticize, or you would ruffle up Malcolm's hair, or you would begin teasing the cat."

"I have never teased a cat in my life, and I was raising cats long before you even thought of being a criminal!" she said hotly.

"Madame Girard."

She began weeping softly.

"If only *one* person cared," she said. "But nobody does. Except perhaps old Mr. Cox. He *does* listen to what I have to say, and he does *not* tell me he loves me when he commands me to do something ridiculous."

"Do you think Mr. Cox would allow you to eat *brioche* in his bed?" Jerome wondered.

"Mr. Cox has never ordered me out of his house." She defended the astrologer.

"Only because you have never been in it," Jerome said acidly.

"Mr. Cox gives me all he can, but he does not pretend he has very much for me. You, like all evangelists, pretend you do."

"You are accusing us of bad faith."

"I am only saying you speak more than you feel."

"We are, then, hypocrites."

"You talk about love a good deal more than you do anything about it, especially you. Or perhaps especially Eloisa." Madame

Girard hesitated. "No, especially both of you. You are professional 'lovers' like the Christians used to be."

"Don't use those terms with regard to us."

"I had forgotten all about how old-fashioned Christians acted until I met you." Madame Girard was firm. "I knew there was some fly in your ointment, but I thought you were a bit soft-brained from prison. But now I know what it is!" she cried in triumph.

"Madame Girard, I'm asking you—" he cried.

"You are an old-fashioned Christian looking for your flock."

"Please," Jerome said, red-faced. "Don't be indecent as well as obnoxious."

Madame Girard rose high in her bed, and slapped him vigorously across the mouth.

"Sit down," she commanded. "I won't have you trying to pretend I am uncontrollable so that you can beat me. Don't I see the sadist in you? Sit down at once."

Jerome sat down, the same deep red on his face.

"I saw through you the day Eloisa married you," Madame Girard told him. "Your honeyed words, your honeyed love. Under all your honey runs a conduit of venom."

"I will not listen to your raving."

"You people who talk and talk about love all the time." Madame Girard ignored his interpolation. "You're the least of the lot. If you did anything about it, you wouldn't have to tell it. I'll bet if I offered you a million dollars right now you would walk out of this room and leave Eloisa on her can. And don't I know why you want Malcolm and Kermit to yourself, too."

Jerome gave her at that moment such a smile of patient condescension and untouchable superiority that Madame Girard's face fell, and she began to weep again.

"You don't love anybody," she sobbed. "You don't love Eloisa, you don't love me, you don't love Malcolm. And you say you're 'cured.' Of what? Cured of everything but talk, that's all, that's the cure, cured to go on your selfish evangelical way acting superior to other human beings and being proud you were a goddamn burglar and can now sit around with your less fortunate straight middle-class fellows, and act superior to them because they are dumb enough to say they don't know to all your pious questions. Yes, you know everything, but wait, just one moment—" and here Madame Girard stood up in the bed and pointed a finger at him with such sternness that the smile on his face slowly disappeared.

"I issue a prognostication on you: your 'cure' is over! Do you hear? You are no longer 'cured.' A long setback is about to overtake you, and you are to go back and learn the lesson you have forgotten from your burglar days, that love is deeds and not honeyed talk."

"And now, Madame Girard," Jerome told her, "will you please get up and get ready to leave, like a good girl?" And he gave her a chaste kiss on her brow.

"Condescension! condescension!" Madame Girard cried. "The last weapon!"

Girard Girard had come, summoned by an intoxicated and distraught Eloisa Brace, and he was waiting, frowning and gray in his handsome raincoat, when Madame Girard came painfully down the long two flights of stairs from the guest room where she had just finished her long interview with Jerome.

Madame Girard stopped at the landing of the second flight of stairs in order to stare at her husband.

"I suppose I have interrupted some *amour* of yours with the kitchen help?" She leveled her attack.

Girard Girard barely looked up from his stance in the middle of the lower room.

"My husband does not speak to me," Madame Girard said to Eloisa Brace, who, standing at the entrance to the room, was weeping and hiccuping.

"Ignored by my own husband, ordered out of the house by a burglar, pommeled by my dearest woman friend—ignored by my beauties," and she waved a gloved hand at each of these persons in succession. "Can anyone deny that my empire is in ruins?"

"Madame Girard," Eloisa cried, going partway up to her.

"Halt!" Madame Girard whispered, and she seized a sprig of greenery which was trailing from a heavy vase.

"I will *not* hear anybody speak of love again," Madame Girard announced. "You are all, yes, all of you, professional love-speakers. Girard Girard, Eloisa, Jerome, the burglar, all of you speak of your great beating love-full hearts. Yet you will not endure my presence here for more than a few hours. You tear me away from the only pleasure that now remains to me in my mature years"—here she threw the sprig of greenery at Girard Girard, on whom it fell as air.

"You call men to come for me whenever you tire of my repetitions, whenever my presence ruffles your comfort, whenever your boredom spouts out of its foundationless depths . . ."

"She is giving the oration," Girard Girard cried in a hopeless voice.

"Yet you," Madame Girard went on, motioning to Girard and Eloisa Brace, "spare yourselves no pleasure. And what would you do if you did not have *me* to talk about, to feel superior to? What pleasure *that* would take away from you! What pleasure indeed!"

She began to weep a little, but then, becoming dry-eyed and mildly savage:

"Without me, your life would have no imagination. For though you cannot stand me in the flesh, my spirit and will are all that keep you going. You are all of you dependent on me for life."

"Christ in heaven!" Girard exclaimed.

"Who has stolen my parasol?" Madame Girard suddenly said in a low voice, like an old actress breaking off at rehearsal.

"Your parasol is here, my dear," Eloisa said, producing it with a swiftness that seemed obscene.

"Ah," Madame Girard cooed. "So you were ready for me . . . You have spared no time at all in having the final preparations for my eviction . . ."

Madame Girard went up close to Eloisa now as if to study a rare stone. Slowly, while Eloisa exchanged looks of fear and doubt with Girard Girard, Madame Girard pressed her lips against Eloisa's forehead, kissing her several times.

Then, looking carefully and critically at Eloisa, Madame Girard said: "You have no beauty left. Your skin, which was never handsome, is now that of a woman without either age or youth. You belong to the nameless waves of the middle-aged."

Eloisa sobbed softly.

"Can any husband looking on that skin feel love?" Madame Girard appealed to the entire room.

There was a long silence.

"Answer my question," Madame Girard commanded Eloisa. "As an artist you are obliged to answer."

Eloisa sat down on the sofa near Girard Girard, and picked up a glass of brandy, which had been left there from the day before.

"Can any man looking at your face see love or even a woman? The answer, my dear Eloisa, is no. You are no longer a woman. Are you an artist indeed? That remains to be seen when the portrait of Malcolm is finished. Are your powers as an artist allied to your powers as a woman? If they are, you are done, finished, through forever."

"Madame Girard," Eloisa cried in great anguish, "you must leave at once."

Girard Girard now advanced toward his wife, galvanized into action by Eloisa's cry.

"Don't touch me, either of you," Madame Girard warned. "I will go out to the car alone, and I will get into it unassisted by anybody. I am leaving this house, of course, forever."

"No, no," Eloisa said. "You will not leave until you promise me you will return in a happier time."

"Eloisa suddenly remembers how very wealthy the both of us are." Madame Girard addressed herself to her husband. She adjusted her scarf about her throat.

"I want, however," Madame Girard added, "I want the portrait of Malcolm, and Girard Girard will pay you for it now."

Eloisa attempted to say something, but her throat had not been sufficiently moistened by the brandy.

"How much is the portrait?" Madame Girard demanded.

"But it is not finished! And you have not seen what is finished!" Eloisa exclaimed.

"How much will it be when finished?" Girard Girard inquired.

Eloisa stood thinking.

"Is five thousand too much to ask?" Eloisa ventured at last.

"Five thousand?" Madame Girard said, beating her parasol into the rug. "Five thousand is not my price for anything."

Girard Girard and Eloisa waited, tense, for her further deliberation.

"Is that price not satisfactory to you, then?" Girard Girard addressed his wife.

"*Five* thousand is not my kind of price for anything, I repeat," Madame Girard expostulated. "Give her ten thousand or nothing."

"Is ten thousand a satisfactory price, Eloisa, my dear?" Girard questioned, looking at the painter warmly and sympathetically.

"Ten thousand," Eloisa gasped, surprised, genuinely surprised.

Girard Girard, however, was already taking out his checkbook.

"But you have not seen the portrait," Eloisa cried weakly. "What if you should not like it?"

Girard Girard meanwhile had written with great rapidity and flourish a check for the amount agreed upon, and handed it now to the painter.

"I have *never* paid five thousand for anything I wanted," Madame Girard warned everybody in the room.

Clapping her hands swiftly, Madame Girard announced, perhaps to cut off the warm looks being exchanged by Girard Girard and Eloisa Brace: "We are leaving."

Going up to Eloisa quickly, Madame Girard kissed her wetly on the mouth and said, "Despite all, you will always be dear to me, Eloisa," and both Madame Girard and Girard Girard left the house at once without another word.

Eloisa's renunciation

"I have been *enriched*!" cried Eloisa Brace. "I am no longer what you can exactly call a pauper, let us say."

Jerome, Malcolm, and Kermit (the latter having, in the confusion, stayed on and *on*)—all three came up to her at that moment like a delegation of congratulation, although her statement had been as private as a soliloquy, and the sight of the check appeared to have removed her from all other human contact.

"Ten thousand smackers!" she moaned.

Singling out Kermit then, Eloisa Brace bent very low and kissed him on the head.

"You are at the pinnacle of your career," Kermit said calmly.

"Thank you, dear," Eloisa replied, all her bitterness against the little man for the present vanished.

"I am the husband of a rich woman," Jerome said, and he was very pale. He sat down on the small wooden chair which Girard Girard had briefly occupied while waiting for Madame Girard to descend.

"Why are you so white?" Eloisa asked her husband, and she

turned also to look at the faces of Malcolm and Kermit, perhaps seeking an explanation of her husband's pallor from them. The two young men, however, both showed pink poker-faces, and of the two, Malcolm showed the lesser emotion. Money, after all, had never been anything special to him, although of late what he had was rapidly dwindling, and had Eloisa said she had just got one million dollars, Malcolm would have probably been just as impressed or unimpressed.

But Jerome knew what money meant, and so Eloisa turned her full attention to him.

"Jerome, dear, you must explain your attitude, and your paleness."

"Must I?" he said, and there was a strange ominous bitterness in his tone.

"What change has come over you?" Eloisa begged to know, and Malcolm saw that her former character of dominance—which he had experienced the night of his arrival—changed now to dependence, almost panic.

When no one spoke, Malcolm began eating a Delicious apple, and his chewing filled the silence.

Eloisa studied Girard Girard's check, meanwhile, admiring the signature, as well as the denomination, and then advancing to the bureau, she took down a purple velvet box, and laid the check inside.

"I wish you would speak, then," Eloisa told Jerome suddenly, her back to him.

"What would you have me speak?" Jerome replied distantly, more distantly than she had ever heard him.

Malcolm's chewing continued.

"It has been a completely full two days," Eloisa remarked after a long silence.

"Ending in wealth for one of us," Jerome commented, with dogged unpleasantness.

"For one of us," Eloisa cried, distracted, and wheeling around at her husband. "What is the meaning of *one*?"

"You heard me say *one,* very well, *one* it is." Jerome raised his voice, and then leaped up, and turning unexpectedly in the direction of Malcolm, he seized the apple almost from out of the boy's mouth and threw it into the fireplace.

"I hate both those goddamn capitalists, the Girards," Jerome cried.

Eloisa Brace began wringing her hands, and Malcolm stared open-mouthed, pieces of apple still unchewed showing on his half-protruding tongue.

Kermit was looking blackly angry in his own corner.

"But you yourself were always wishing for money," Eloisa expostulated. "And they paid it for a *painting*."

"They did not, and you know they did not," roared Jerome.

"Oh, my darling," Eloisa Brace said, and she went up to her husband and put her head on his shoulder.

Jerome roughly shook her off, saying, "Stand over there with the boys, and don't act a role which you don't feel."

Eloisa went obediently to the part of the room where the boys were stationed. Malcolm had picked up his apple, dusted it off, and was again chewing, and Eloisa could not help but place a warning finger against his mouth.

"I wish you would explain it all to me, dear Jerome." Eloisa attempted to soothe him from her new position in the room.

"Why should I explain what is crystal clear?" Jerome said tensely. "Madame Girard has no high opinion of you as an artist."

"But the tribute of the money," Eloisa gasped, struggling not to hear more.

"Must I tell you in *primer* terms?" Jerome cried.

"I am afraid primer terms are required," she said, after thinking a moment.

"You wish brutality, I guess," Jerome emphasized to her.

"I want things said, yes, I do," Eloisa said with more vigor than she had employed up to now.

"Madame Girard, like many in our circle, is infatuated with Malcolm," and here Jerome pointed to the boy in question, and Malcolm half-rose, bowed slightly, and swallowed the remains of his apple.

"Oh, but Jerome," Eloisa begged him. "There had to be a

picture, after all, whoever the subject: it is the picture that matters!"

"Of course there had to be a picture," Jerome said with menacing sweetness.

"Then all is settled: all is settled, and well," Eloisa urged on him.

"All is not settled, and nothing will ever be well between us again," Jerome called out to her, livid with anger.

"How familiar and complete this all is," Kermit said, suddenly coming out from his corner.

"Be silent at once, and don't play any role in this, *Kermit*." Eloisa turned on him.

Kermit showed his teeth in his well-known sardonic silent laugh.

"Why is *nothing* settled?" Eloisa turned to the argument with her husband.

"That money is a bribe and nothing more. By accepting the money," Jerome cried, and in his excitement his spittle sprinkled itself upon his wife's face—"by accepting the money, you not only proclaim to the world that you have ceased to be a serious artist (which Madame Girard believes anyhow), you have given her, to quote one of her phrases, *carte blanche* to enter this house at any time she escapes from her husband's surveillance. And she probably thinks she owns Malcolm, too —although he may be as disgustingly wealthy as she and her crooked financier husband, for all I know."

Malcolm now stepped forward to say something, but Eloisa pushed him rudely (he thought) back into the corner with Kermit.

"Then, as usual, all I have done, and all I have attempted is a mistake," Eloisa summarized their discussion.

"I am speaking of the situation; I have not come to you as yet," Jerome replied.

"But I have created this situation. Where is your honesty if you pretend now I am innocent of anything?"

"You have accepted money on false premises."

"Then what is your wish and decision in the case?"

Eloisa held out her arms to him in a token of resignation.

"There can be only one decision," Jerome told her.

Eloisa stood watching him, pale as he was now, and when he did not say any more immediately, she turned her back on him, and went to the sideboard, took down the brandy bottle, and poured herself a generous draught.

"Don't drink . . . quite yet," he asked her.

"I must have a drink to hear what it is you are going to say."

"You do not know what I am going to say." Jerome was savage again.

"There is nobody in this room so feebleminded he does not know what you are going to say," she cried.

"What I was about to say, Eloisa, is—you drink as much as Madame Girard," her husband said to her.

"And you have come to the point of moralizing more than Mr. Cox," Eloisa retorted.

"Mr. Cox was mentioned," Malcolm cried to Kermit.

"Silence." Eloisa turned on the boy again. "Be silent or leave the room!"

"Will you control yourself?" Jerome sang out to her, and he went over to his wife and took the brandy glass out of her hand.

"You will allow me, then, no deadening of the pain to come," Eloisa said.

"You have not only betrayed yourself," Jerome said, "you have cheapened our marriage."

"Yes, it is always I, *I*, who am low, and you, *you* with your years of suffering who are noble."

Kermit laughed aloud at that moment from his corner, but nobody thought to correct him.

"Tell me, then, what your impossible wishes are," Eloisa said in a stifled voice to her husband. "Tell me or be silent."

"Eloisa," Jerome said in his quiet firm voice, the voice he had used to convince Madame Girard that she must leave the house, "you know perfectly well it is you who must tell me."

"I knew you would say that," and Eloisa folded her arms across her breast.

"I shall sit down, now"—Jerome was calm—"and wait for your statement."

"I will break under the pressure some day, and then you will regret some things," Eloisa warned him, but without conviction, and she went to the brandy bottle again, and drank directly out of it this time.

"An Amazon out of her period," Kermit exclaimed in a loud voice to Malcolm, who seemed to have fallen into one of his sleepy attitudes, and did not appear too attentive to what was transpiring.

"I am to tell you, then, what it is I am to do," Eloisa began again.

"I will not open my mouth until the right decision has been made." Jerome was unshakable.

"Must my life *always* be heroic?" Eloisa said with routine bitterness. "Is there to be no rest anywhere, no oasis in the . . ."

She opened her arms again to Jerome, but he turned away gloomily.

"How can I say what you want me to say?" she appealed again to him.

"You must choose between me and the rich. The decision is simple." He broke his own silence.

"My nature is more complicated than your decision, I fear," Eloisa said.

"A choice, however, must be made," he warned her again.

"Why did it have to happen? Why did I have to *see* the money, then—to know its pleasure—only to give it up?"

"You're actually going to give up money, then?" Malcolm said, opening his eyes from the half-slumber into which he had been plunged.

Eloisa let out cries of pain on this remark, and Jerome admonished Malcolm to silence.

But Malcolm whispered with Kermit, and Kermit nodded, and laughed softly.

"Were there ever two such days of pain for me in a row?" Eloisa cried. She looked momentarily and savagely in the direction of the boys, and then, going up directly to the little velvet box, she took out the check which Girard Girard had signed with such a flourish only an hour before.

She held the paper before her an instant, like one who sees more written on it now than she had at first discovered, and then suddenly tearing it all up before them, she tossed the pieces into her mouth, and began chewing them.

"Eloisa!" Malcolm cried, going up to her.

Jerome stood up now, and commanded, a benign expression coming over his recent scowl—"Let her alone. Let her do what she must."

She ate a bit more of the check, and then seeing Jerome so close to her, she struck him soundly over the jaw. He was silent, like a man perfunctorily measuring the precise force of the blow.

Kermit broke loose now in uncontrolled laughter.

"You're all of a pack!" Eloisa cried out suddenly, looking at all of them. "You're all fairies, that's what. All a pack of fairies. And you let women carry the burden, while all you do is talk. Damn all of you! Fairies! Fairies!" she cried, weeping, and seizing the brandy bottle, she ran out of the room.

"Leave me Madame Girard"

During his courtship of her, many years before, Girard Girard and Madame Girard had often sat in a dark wood on the other side of the lagoon from the Japanese Temples, but still within earshot of the bench on which Malcolm was later to sit. Girard Girard had here asked her to marry him, and she had, of course, refused.

Another few days had passed, and Fall shaking down the last leaves, he had asked her again. This time, silently weeping over her passing youth, she could not speak but nodded rather vigorously for a woman of her temperament. Girard Girard, like the magician he was, already holding the ring in the palm of his hand, pushed it with painful vigor onto her finger, and kissed her heavily on her mouth. (The trap opened and closed, as she told Mr. Cox later, and all old and dear things were forever replaced by marriage.)

"You are then victorious," Madame Girard had said to her husband-to-be.

"We are both victorious," he told her with what she knew was excessive pride.

"What kind of victory can that be?" she cried, amazed. "What kind of victory is it in which we are *both* winners?"

It was then that Girard Girard knew, if he had not known before, that marriage with her would be a continuous contest.

"There must be victories for both," he told her, "if there is to be victory for one."

"But victory has always been only *my own*," she countered, "unshared with another. A victory shared would be somebody else's, not my own."

She looked at her ring with surprise now.

He waited for a reply to occur to him, shuffling his feet on the oak leaves that formed a carpet for their interview.

"I am always alone in victory," she exclaimed, frightened at the changes that now suddenly appeared about her on all sides, like cracks in an ice floe.

"You are no longer unprotected, no longer alone is all." Girard Girard kissed her again on the mouth.

"My real victories cannot be shared," she insisted to him. "No one understands my victories."

"You cannot forbid me to rejoice in your success," Girard said, and he touched the finger on which he had placed the ring.

"I can forbid you to feign you are rejoicing over my success, but I will not," she explained. "I will be generous."

"Thank you," he replied, nodding.

They both stood up, and he embraced her. She gave no sign of acquiescence or happiness.

"Now we are together," he said, more pleading than asserting.

She was silent.

"May I not now call you Madame Girard, which you always said you would forbid me to call you until you had said yes?"

She forced down his arms from where they had held her, and looking past him to where the trees stood nearly naked over the lagoon, she said, "I will now be Madame Girard to the entire world. I will be no one else."

No one had ever addressed her again by anything except that name.

~~~

Madame Girard recalled these things to herself, almost aloud, from that long yesterday afternoon, while she listened intermittently to Girard Girard entertain her at the piano. He played Scarlatti tolerably well, and he was playing him now to quiet her.

"In a little while you will go out to commit your routine adulteries," she said to him above his playing.

"And," she continued, unsure whether he had heard her or not, "while you embrace laundresses and chambermaids, I am deprived of the sight of Malcolm, before whom I only wish to light candles. My loves have always been of that type. The candle-lighting type."

Madame Girard, who had never loved and perhaps never respected Girard Girard, now suddenly whetted her own interest in him as a result of his incessant unfaithfulness to her. She sometimes followed him now in a taxi to simulate attention and desire, and as she watched him meet a woman and drive off with her speedily to some second-class hotel, she felt a kind of slow distant imitation of love that should have come to her full-force the afternoon long past when he had put the ring on her hand.

She observed his animal vigor as it descended into his hands on the piano keys.

"The music, like all else he touches," she said aloud, but inaudible to his ears, "is but the overture to his sexual perfection with women."

But a thought that had come to her even before the afternoon of the lagoon had been recurring to her now with a kind of feathered swiftness, like that of a poisoned arrow which, she knew, would this time leave its fatal mark.

She had never loved Girard, and Girard, of course, had never precisely loved her as a woman. He had worshipped her, satisfying his appetite with the blossoming bodies of common women, but (and here the feathered arrow whizzed horribly about her ears) his worship had grown with the years. As she lighted candles to handsome young men like Malcolm, he had never ceased keeping a whole altar of lights burning to her. Now suddenly (and here she felt the poison of the arrow strike her) he would no longer light candles to her. The last match had been put to the last wick.

Girard Girard no longer loved Madame Girard.

And within a few days, or hours, or months, she knew, he would take the title from her. She would have no name. Another Madame Girard would replace her.

"Stop!" she cried suddenly, and she threw a candelabrum at him as he still sat at the piano.

He waited there, flushed with some new emotion, the candelabrum having missed him by inches.

"You hit a wrong note," she explained, and they both knew she said this as a lie, even though he *had* hit a wrong note.

He got up without a word, and this was the first time her shaken mind recognized that *it* had finally occurred.

He put on his great coat, which he wore only for the most crucial of business deals.

"No, Girard," she expostulated, and at that moment, they both recognized victory passed forever from her to him.

"Girard Girard!" she cried, going up to him.

Now he took *her* arms and put them down away from him.

"Do not look to me," he said, and immediately he had said these words, he trembled, shaken with the power of his own excommunication of her.

"I will kill myself this time," she said.

"That, dear child, is your choice." He stood like stone before her, and the depth of his gaze never left him. He was granite, she saw, with his new character, his new and complete victory.

"You will have to look at me as I lie crushed and bleeding," she said, but almost to herself now, because she knew he was going out of her life altogether.

"Madame Girard, you must for this one time listen to reason," he said finally, and for a moment, and a moment only, he threw back his heavy coat with the colored silk lining on which his name blazoned like a shield.

Her eyes fell on the intense gold letters of his identification, seeing perhaps then her own identity melting away into the letters of his name.

"Girard Girard," she pleaded. "I mean to kill myself."

"You remember, your victories were all to be your own." He recalled the lagoon for her.

"That was *then*," she insisted, like a woman he had never known.

"This is now." Girard commanded by his tone.

"I will not, of course, kill myself merely to please you," she began.

"You are free to do what you can and what you must. When I walk out of here tonight, I will walk out forever."

"But victory is always mine," she now echoed him, hollowly. "Do you not recognize me?" she inquired, a new kind of wildness in her face. "I am Madame Girard."

He advanced now like an actor in an overlengthy unsuccessful play who is about to make a speech after which the curtain must fall precipitously upon his last syllable.

"You are no longer Madame Girard," he said.

She faced him now without defense, wordless, with the expression of almost any woman, his laundress, his charwoman.

"You have ceased to exist," he told her.

"I am not . . . Madame Girard?" she whispered.

"When I go out of this house, I will not return. I go out this time to *be* married."

"You cannot know marriage," she cried. "I forbid you, and you cannot know it anyhow."

She laughed unsteadily, and going over to a closed cabinet, she opened the door, and looking back in mild defiance, she drew out a small pistol.

He made no motion to stop her.

"I will always be Madame Girard. A command from you cannot destroy my identity."

"I am issuing no command in this case, as you yourself must see," he told her.

She stared at the pistol.

"You are the one, my dear, who has ceased to be Madame Girard. I have not touched you," he said finally.

"How could I cease to be she! Was I not she last night when you wrote the ten-thousand-dollar check for Eloisa Brace?"

"It was your last night of existence," he explained.

She half-leveled the pistol at him.

"I am divorcing you in order to marry Laureen Raphaelson."

Madame Girard raised the hand with the pistol like one who may command an entire army to extinguish itself, and then, letting her hand drop before she gave the omnipotent gesture, she exclaimed, weak and without humor: "The wife of the midget."

"We have found one another," he said, picking up the pistol, which she had let fall to the floor, and placing it on top of a reading desk.

"I will not allow you to degrade yourself," she began. "You can marry *anybody* else. I will urge you, in fact, to marry a woman of your class. But I will not allow you . . . her."

Suddenly the idea came to her: "And *she* will be Madame Girard?"

"She will indeed," he replied.

"But you could so much easier change *your* names than I mine," she begged.

"You forget who bestowed his name on you. And you have never realized that *all the time*"—and here he advanced almost threateningly upon her—"that victory was always mine. I *am* victory."

She bent under the words.

"You are victory now," she admitted. "But I will destroy you . . ."

"And through what?" he cried.

"Through a beautiful young man."

He laughed.

"I am Madame Girard," she went on. "The whole world has always known me as she, the whole world will not so quickly lose its memory."

"The world remembers only what power and money tell it."

He spoke to her like one who merely reads from a document. "And my power and money now decree that you no longer exist."

"Victory has always been mine," she repeated incoherently.

"That was in the lagoon, in the days when I had this strange love for you. And strange it was," he laughed.

"Girard Girard," she cried. "Patience, pity. I can change!"

"There is a limit to time and fortune," he said. "You are now —history."

"But without my name, without your fortune," she cried.

"My dear"—he made a gesture of writing—"you will continue to be wealthy."

A cool pity came into his voice. "You will be comfortable, richly entertained. You will be able to see your 'beauties.' "

"But my name!" she cried. "I am known everywhere as Madame Girard."

"Your name must be taken from you. Has already *been* taken."

"You mean to destroy my identity, then?"

"Your friends, your young men, will come to see what is you. Your pure victory, as you have always called it, is now. You are completely free—can't you see?"

"But I need the name. The name is mine."

"It is too late," he said. "Laureen is waiting for me. We have so much to discuss. And there is so little time for the kind of happiness I know I can have with her."

"My name! You cannot take it. Take the money, the victory, but leave me as I was: Madame Girard."

"Fate has already moved. You speak as the melancholy young woman should have spoken on the lagoon so long, long ago."

"Girard Girard," she pleaded and she went down on her knees to him.

"It has been a week of melodrama," he said, fatigued. "A lifetime of melodrama."

He buttoned his great coat.

"Your shoes are so beautifully shined," she wept.

Suddenly she kissed his shoes.

"Leave me with what I was," she begged. "Leave me *Madame Girard*."

She saw the shoes withdraw from her embrace, and a moment later she heard the closing of the massive outside door.

At the horticultural gardens

Very early in the morning, while still sleeping heavily in a large bed on the third floor which he shared with three musicians, Malcolm was awakened by Eloisa Brace.

"Girard Girard has asked that you come at once to see him at the horticultural gardens," she cried.

Malcolm opened his eyes slowly and gaped at her.

She repeated this news to the grumbling and complaint of the three musicians, one of whom wore a silk stocking over his head as a night cap, and all of whom had actually only just turned in a few minutes before and just gotten nicely to sleep.

"It is very important for your future, Malcolm," Eloisa Brace went on. "You MUST go to see him."

Malcolm looked at her, uncomprehending.

"Remember, your money is going, you have given up your hotel suite, and your father will not return from the dead."

"But my portrait!" Malcolm cried.

"There is no portrait now, kiddy," Eloisa said solemnly. "Remember?"

"You are turning me out bag and baggage?" the boy cried.

"For Christ almighty's sake!" The musician with the silk stocking on his head raised up, enraged at the disturbance.

"Shh, come immediately, Malcolm," Eloisa said. "You have no choice. O.K.? No choice at all in the matter."

She hurried him to the bathroom, where he put on his clothes, and downstairs in her basement kitchen she hurriedly gave him a cup of coffee with milk, and then took him to the curb, where she hailed a taxi.

She kissed him goodbye.

"I am not turning you out, Malcolm—I am turning you over to stronger hands. Please remember that we love you, Jerome and I. But when all is said and done, Malcolm, kiddy, you are not in our class. O.K.? I hope I do not offend. And I really feel that Girard Girard has the key to your future."

"But the bench and all," Malcolm expostulated, as he was put into the cab. "Kermit . . . And Mr. Cox . . . And yes, even Estel Blanc . . ."

"You will see them again, Malcolm, when better days come to us all," Eloisa said to him from behind the pane of glass of the taxi.

"Goodbye and good luck, for you will need it," she cried. "We are just not of your class," she repeated, as the taxi drove off.

As it began to disappear with the boy, she sighed, relief and hope coming into her eyes.

"Destination?" the chauffeur inquired, but Malcolm was groaning in the back seat with sleep, confusion and despair, and did not reply.

"You said something?" Malcolm finally addressed himself to the driver.

The chauffeur repeated his question.

"Why"—Malcolm thought for a while—"the horticultural gardens, I believe she said. Did you not hear the lady say that?" he inquired.

"I believe I did, sir," the driver responded.

"I'm leaving everything behind!" Malcolm told the driver.

"And I don't know any other part of the city at all . . . My hotel, my bench, Mr. Cox, Kermit, Jerome, the piano player—everything behind!" he cried out, inconsolable.

Girard Girard came out from the entrance of the horticultural gardens when he heard the approach of the taxi, paid the driver, and helped Malcolm down from the cavernous back seat.

He ushered the boy into the first room of the greenhouse, which was devoted to tropical plants.

"I called you here, Malcolm," Girard Girard said, "only because you are, I know, my friend. I hope that you consider yourself my friend also, despite the fantastic difference in our ages and our respective positions in life."

Girard Girard motioned to the boy to sit down on a stone chair, which appeared to be the only article of furniture in the tropical garden.

"I am therefore appealing to you, Malcolm," Girard Girard said to the boy.

Perhaps owing to the heavy sultry heat of the horticultural gardens, or to the shock at his break with his life, Malcolm was slow to extend his sympathy to the older man, or respond to his speech of welcome, for the boy said nothing at all, and finally, in an attempt to suppress his yawning, he hiccuped loudly in the mossy silence of the gardens.

"Are you going to reject me, too, Malcolm?"

Malcolm stared at the cavernous circles which surrounded Girard's eyes, adding ten years to his age. He looked like a handsome but demolished angel.

"Reject you, sir?"

"Malcolm," the older man said at once, "I have left Madame Girard."

"Left her?" The boy hiccuped again.

"Shall I call an attendant for some water?" Girard inquired, somewhat irritably.

Malcolm shook his head.

"Our twenty years of life together—Madame Girard's and

mine—are at an end," Girard impressed upon the boy's mind.

Malcolm nodded, holding his hand tightly against his throat to prevent another hiccup.

"But I have left her—only because—*only because* I am to be married."

"My congratulations, sir." Malcolm bowed slightly.

"Malcolm," the older man said, looking searchingly into the boy's face, "do you understand what I am saying to you?"

The boy nodded, then smiled.

"You are so winning," the older man almost complained. "But do you *know,* do you *hear,* do you *comprehend*? Oh, how I need you at this moment. Need somebody. I am entirely, entirely alone," he cried.

"Sir," Malcolm began again.

"No, don't speak," the older man said. "I don't say this in anger, but in despair. Malcolm, you do NOT understand . . ."

"I do, sir, I do . . . And I try!"

"You don't understand, Malcolm, and perhaps that is why, well, I need you more than anybody else. For though I am to be married—almost indeed at once—I need you and I mean to have you . . . Madame Girard shall not have you to herself!"

Malcolm opened his mouth to reply to this, but Girard was already speaking again:

"I am going to marry Laureen Raphaelson, Malcolm."

"Laureen . . . The little man's *woman*?"

Malcolm hiccuped.

"Woman?" Girard Girard flushed.

"Forgive me, sir," Malcolm said. "I only met Laureen once, you see, and that was the evening before she went off with the . . . Japanese wrestler."

"Oh, that old story. An invention of Mr. Cox."

"I only know, of course, what people tell me," Malcolm explained.

"Malcolm, you *are* of my class, and you must understand a man's principles: one does not marry a woman because she is a virgin."

The boy agreed gravely.

"You see, Malcolm, with Laureen I will be the father of children: sons will come after me who will bear my name. While with Madame Girard our future was only our present, our future was only . . . well, Madame Girard!

"But you prefer Madame Girard to me, is that not it?" Girard asked, looking intently at the boy's eyes.

"No," Malcolm said in a choked and rather old voice. "I prefer you, Girard Girard. You were my favorite address. Only, I think of you and Madame Girard as together, and when you will be apart . . . I don't know yet what to say."

"You see, Malcolm—and you must already know this—Madame Girard has expressed the wish, ahead of everybody else, to have you. My desires in this matter were, I admit, second. But what I have brought you here for is to ask you as humbly as possible, if you will not . . . choose *me* instead of her."

"Choose you for what, sir?"

"For my own—for Laureen's and my own."

"Oh, sir!"

"I will be your *father* if necessary, though I know that is something that would be difficult . . ."

"No, no." The boy stood up. "There was only one father," Malcolm said sternly, his eyes flashing. "You may be great, but you will not take the place that he occupied alone and first."

"Malcolm, I have no desire to offend your father's memory."

"Your desire was not asked, sir," Malcolm said. "You replace nobody."

"I have put it awkwardly, Malcolm. Kindly reconsider . . ."

Suddenly a violent hiccup came from Mr. Girard's interlocutor.

"Please be seated again, Malcolm, and let us be calm."

The boy sat down.

"We will begin again, if necessary, all over." Girard Girard paced up and down in front of the stone chair.

Malcolm muttered something between his teeth, but the look of intensity on his face was so incredible at that moment that

Girard Girard took out a handkerchief from his breast pocket and wiped his face carefully.

"In all humbleness, Malcolm," the older man began again, "consider my offer."

"But what is your offer, sir?" The boy was severe.

"Come live with me and my new wife, accept all we have to offer, feel secure and loved with us. Ask whatever you wish of us."

"But I had everything until just a few days ago," the boy cried. "And suddenly, having left the bench entirely . . . for reasons I do not recall—I have *nothing.*"

"But you have me. You have us."

"I have lost everything!" the boy said, and then his violence disintegrated into a sudden calm and even sweetness.

"You will not come with me, then?" Girard Girard said.
Malcolm shook his head.

"You wish to go to Madame Girard?" the older man wondered, somewhat stupefied.

"No, no," the boy responded.

"But then what are you going to do? You cannot go back to your hotel suite. It is rented . . . And no longer being a pensioner there, so to speak, I fear the bench is barred to you likewise . . ."

The boy shifted in his hard seat. Perhaps at last the realization of his position became clear, for turning to his would-be protector, he demanded:

"Would you repeat what you just said, please, Girard Girard?"

"I will repeat anything you may wish," the older man said. "However, I have forgotten my exact words . . ."

"You said, I believe, sir, that I had nothing to go back to!"

"Ah, yes, of course. You see, I have this wedding on my mind—not to mention the tiresome affair of the divorce. Of course, I remember . . . It was simply that the hotel can never take you back, as I said."

"I am barred from it?"

"Well, not barred, but that expensive period of your life is simply over, dear boy. As over and done with as those days when your father came home from a long business trip and tucked you in at night. You're nearly grown up!"

"Grown up? Why, then, whatever will I do?"

"You can go ahead alone, of course," and here Girard Girard gave the boy a look of pity mixed with horror, "or you can come with me, and allow me to open all doors for you."

"All doors," Malcolm repeated.

Going up to Malcolm now in a manner uncommon for the financier, he seized the boy by the shoulders vigorously and shaking him, said:

"You can't go on by yourself!"

"But what if Mr. Cox should give me more addresses!" the boy got out while still being shaken.

"More addresses!" Girard exclaimed, letting loose the boy. "Do you know what you are talking about? Obviously not. Then listen: Mr. Cox *has* no more addresses . . ."

"No more at all?"

"Not a single one. No, that old dodge is out. And besides, how could he give them to you when you're so friendly to me? And besides!" But here Girard stopped, owing to the look of panic on the boy's face.

But he continued anyhow, despite Malcolm's expression: "And besides," he finished, "Mr. Cox would hardly give you another address since *you are off the bench*."

"Off the bench!" the boy cried, realization pouring into his eyes.

"Choose me, dear Malcolm. Choose us."

"A wedding," the boy mused. "And so many things, so many ways!"

"Tell me your answer is yes."

Malcolm nodded, gravely smiling.

"I knew you would give in," Girard cried, happy. "I will make things up to you, let me tell you. And I will try never to replace anybody either. I have learned my lesson there, too."

Malcolm sat back now on the stone chair.

"But I have not a minute," Girard Girard told him. "A most

important engagement. I must leave at once. But you stay here, Malcolm, for I will be back in an hour at the most to pick you up. Don't go away, do you hear? Now that I've found you, I don't want to lose you for anything, you see."

"Please do not go away without me." Malcolm stood up, and Girard Girard had never heard the boy speak with such strength, though his voice cracked a little, for it was changing. "Take me with you."

"Quite out of the question," Girard told him. "My engagement is of the utmost importance, and you would only be in the way. Stay here, as I say, and within the hour I will be back again. And we will both begin life together!"

Malcolm smiled.

The two friends shook hands, and in another moment, Girard Girard had left Malcolm to thoughts and expectancy.

Malcolm meets a contemporary

Malcolm waited in the horticultural gardens.

An hour passed, then two. He grew hungry, but he saw no place where he could get anything to eat.

For a while he strolled about the grounds, always being careful to be within earshot of the stone chair on which Girard Girard expected to find him on his return.

But after a while, the shadows of evening began to fall, and still no sign of his great and powerful friend.

At five o'clock, an attendant appeared, informing the boy that the horticultural gardens were about to close.

Malcolm waited therefore outside the building on the greensward, but in a short while another attendant informed him that this was not allowed, as the entire grounds were about to be closed, and that he should go out through the gate and stand on the sidewalk near the arterial, if he was waiting for somebody.

"But Girard Girard is expecting me *here*!" Malcolm told the attendant.

The attendant, who recognized immediately the name pronounced by the boy, thought for a moment, then said:

"But he would never return now! It is not his way. You had better go at once to his house."

"He has no house now that he has left Madame Girard," the boy replied.

The attendant clicked his tongue.

Malcolm was already walking in the direction of the sidewalk and the arterial. As he reached the walk, he heard from behind the closing of the tall gates of the horticultural gardens, and the snap as they locked themselves against him.

Standing waiting there, Malcolm was surprised at how quickly night came, and a cool breeze from the west reminded him that summer was over.

"Girard Girard," he muttered bitterly.

Malcolm leaned against a telephone pole which was covered with posters announcing the appearance in the neighborhood of a popular singing star. He perhaps dozed a little, then was awakened by the sound of a motorcycle whizzing past. When the motorcycle had gone past him, it stopped suddenly, wheeled about dizzily on its own tracks, and returned dead level to Malcolm. The driver, who was even darker than Estel Blanc or George Leeds, stopped, removed his goggles, and opened his mouth to say something to Malcolm, but at the very last second, did not speak at all, merely showing his even ivory teeth.

Malcolm took, therefore, the initiative, and wished the motorcyclist a good evening.

"You one of the contemporaries?" the motorcyclist said, not replying to Malcolm's greeting.

Malcolm said he begged his pardon.

"If you one of the contemporaries, get on behind me, and we'll go right over to Melba's, and if you ain't, it don't matter too awful much anyhow, on account of you is the type."

Malcolm was about to tell the motorcyclist that he was waiting for Girard Girard, but with the command "Stow it!" the boy next found himself behind the motorcyclist headed away from the city, in a whirlpool of rushing air.

Occasionally he would hear the name Melba come from the driver's mouth, blown to him by a torrent of air, but the rest of the man's words were carried away by other currents, and never reached him. And Malcolm was too downcast and even embittered by Girard Girard's failure to show up to feel any wrongdoing in leaving the horticultural gardens. Apparently Girard Girard was more interested in his coming wedding and his present divorce than he was in Malcolm, and with Mr. Cox and the addresses and the bench and Kermit all swallowed up in the past, he was more than pleased that he could be driving off with someone like this who showed every friendly intention and interest in him personally. And the new driver had a most pleasing perfume of nasturtiums about him, together with a voice which, while not perhaps as rich as the baritone depth of Estel Blanc's, was much more warm and friendly.

After driving very fast for a good many miles, during which the entire landscape flashed past them, a soft dissolving mass, the motorcyclist brought the vehicle to a dizzying halt at a gasoline pump, which had no attendant, and which was not illuminated clearly.

Taking out a small flashlight from his hip pocket, the motorcyclist with his other hand held a key to the gasoline pump, and having opened the pump, proceeded to fill his tank, and then seeing the quizzical look on Malcolm's face, said:

"This here tank belongs to Melba and the contemporaries."

Before Malcolm again had time to inquire about Melba and the contemporaries, they were again flashing through the landscape.

After another hour or more of travel, they drew up to a roadhouse, which bore no sign of life of any kind, and appeared without the faintest illumination.

"If you need to fresh yourself up, you can go back there." The driver pointed in the direction of a clump of trees behind the roadhouse.

Malcolm shook his head.

"You *is* a contemporary?" the motorcyclist asked with a sudden desire for confirmation.

Malcolm was about to answer, but the driver had already turned away from him, headed for the door of the roadhouse, and said:

"Melba will know anyhow if you is or isn't."

They now opened the heavy front door and walked into a small room, where ten or twelve men and women were seated drinking, while a very young woman, standing on a platform, was singing to them.

"That one singing there is Melba," the motorcyclist pointed out to Malcolm.

Melba stopped singing briefly to examine the two new arrivals, her eye resting a long time on Malcolm, then questioningly on the motorcyclist, and finally she nodded to the latter, and made a quick gesture with her hand.

"You made it!" The motorcyclist slapped Malcolm on the cheek with vigor, and then shook hands with him.

"Another contemporary!" the driver announced to the people who were seated listening to Melba, who had again begun to sing, some of the words drifting over to where Malcolm and the motorcyclist stood:

> *When you said goodbye, dark daddy,*
> *Did you know I had not yet said hello?*

Malcolm and the driver sat down at a table to wait for Melba to finish her number, after which, Malcolm was informed, she would join them, and give them some pointers about what they could do next.

A young man wearing a tight sash about his middle came up just then and asked them what drink they wished to choose.

"Do you have a preferential?" the driver asked Malcolm, and when the latter said that at the moment he did not, the driver told the man with the sash to bring the usual.

"I'm so glad I didn't make a mistake when I done drew you," the driver told Malcolm. "What if you hadn't been the right one waiting there?" he laughed.

He seemed so much happier and relaxed now that he told Malcolm his name, Gus.

"Who are you?" Gus wanted to know next.

"Malcolm," the boy replied.

"What a non-usual name," Gus commented.

Their drinks arrived, and Gus said that they should toast the contemporaries, and they both raised their glasses briefly.

When you said goodbye—

—the final notes now poured forth from Melba's throat, and in a sea of applause she trod directly through the audience to the table at which Gus and Malcolm were waiting for her.

"Meet a contemporary," Gus told Melba with some excitement.

"Of course, Brownie, of course," Melba said impatiently. "I recognized him im-med-i-ate-ly. He's just about my age category."

Malcolm looked at Melba more closely, and he was surprised and pleased to notice that actually she was *not* much older than he.

While Melba ordered a drink from the boy in the sash, Gus whispered in Malcolm's ear: "She worth her weight in cash. She *terribly* rich."

"Quit whispering, Brownie," Melba told Gus. She took Malcolm's hand in hers.

"What if he hadn't been a contemporary, huh?" Gus laughed nervously now, exchanging a look with Melba.

Malcolm was about to ask them what a contemporary was, but suddenly his old desire to ask questions deserted him. He found that he did not care now what anything was. Too much had happened, too many people had come and gone in his life, and feeling a sudden warmth and pressure from Melba's hand, he mechanically brought this hand to his lips and kissed it.

"I have had such a short long life," Malcolm said, meaning this remark to be silent and for himself, but by accident the words came out loud and strong, and Melba, extremely pleased by what he had said, immediately drank a toast to him.

"I could marry you," she told Malcolm.

Malcolm pressed her hand again.

"You can't get married again, Melba," Gus told her. "Think of—"

"That will do, Brownie," Melba said. And when Gus began to speak again, she cried, "I SAY!"

Gus looked down at his drink, and Melba explained more softly, "Brownie was my first husband. Old Number One, as we sometimes call him."

"I'm not ashamed of it, Melba," Gus said.

"I'm so glad he found you." Melba turned again to Malcolm, and she kissed him warmly on his mouth. "Do you think you could find happiness with me?" Melba said.

Malcolm was suddenly sure. "Yes," he said, "Melba, I do."

"Isn't it all wonderful?" Melba turned briefly to Gus. "Are you sulking again?" she criticized the driver.

When he did not answer, she posed her question:

"Would you marry me, Malcolm?"

"It's too sudden," Gus told Melba. "Wait till Tuesday."

"What in God's name is Tuesday to me." She was highly critical of Gus again. "I gave up the days of the week after Freddie's time, and after you did all those dirty legal things to me . . . Why should Tuesday matter?" she complained, angry tears in her eyes.

Melba pressed Malcolm's hand again.

"You're the first real find Gus has ever made," Melba explained to Malcolm, her lip quivering still a bit. "Do you really care for me?" she inquired now of Malcolm after a pause in which they had all finished their drinks.

"I do, Melba," Malcolm replied, and he did. Having lost Girard Girard and Mr. Cox, Kermit, and the bench, he held more tightly to Melba than he had ever held to any other human being, with the exception, of course, of his father.

"Melba, I DO!" Malcolm cried suddenly, and he kissed the girl on her throat.

"I've never been so quickly surprised, or so quickly happy!" Melba began, but at a look from Gus she began complaining again: "You begrudge me this happiness, don't you? Answer me, don't you? You begrudge me this tiny tiny bit of happiness in my life of pettiness and struggle . . ."

"Melba, honey, happiness is the last thing I *be*-grudge you," Gus told her. "But I don't want you to rush into matrimony this here time. Think of how many other old times you done got stung. Think of the courts, Melba, honey."

"He begrudges me," Melba explained to Malcolm.

"How did you know he was a contemporary?" Melba inquired suspiciously of Gus now, cocking her head in the direction of Malcolm.

"I have *some* tendencies!" Gus became somewhat riled.

"I think it was all just a . . . a beautiful accident . . . for which you don't have no thanks or credit coming!" Melba cried, and her false eyelashes waved in the tempest of her breath.

Gus put his fists in his eyes and said goddamn it all to hell, she would try to take away his credit.

"All right, all right," Melba said apologetically to Gus. "I will give you this credit. I won't harp needlessly on things that can't be proved. You found this baby, and I will be eternally grateful to you. Eternally."

She patted Malcolm's hand.

"God, we will be happy," she whispered. "Everything will be taken care of." She winked, omniscient.

Malcolm made a sound, which resembled a coo, and which he had never heard come from himself before, so that he sat up straight, startled.

"Isn't he *beautiful*, Brownie?" Melba called Gus's attention to the boy now. "Have you noticed his three dimples when he smiles?"

Gus made the strange little groaning sounds again, and began to put his fists in his eyes, then put them down manfully on the table with a bang.

"But *you're* beautiful, Melba," Malcolm was telling her. "You're . . . the beautiful one!"

"Nobody has said that to me since I was twelve." Melba dabbed at her cheek briefly with her napkin.

Gus covered his eyes with his palm now.

"If you feel you want to marry me, dearest," Melba told Malcolm, "we can have Gus here announce it. Everybody here, almost, is a contemporary."

"Melba, sweet Jesus!" Gus cried in a voice which had broken to falsetto.

"Resume your normal baritone when you wish to communicate with me." Melba spoke to Gus.

"Malcolm"—Melba turned her full attention to him again—"I don't even care if you are a contemporary or not. Of course, I knew Gus lied to me about you. But I'm willing to marry you if you are willing to marry me. I've simply got it is all, it's come like lightning, and . . . well, I've been got."

"He ain't OLD ENOUGH!" Gus cried, in his regular voice now.

"Don't listen to him," Melba said, tapping on the marble of the table. "Besides, everything is always arranged. Brownie feels he has to be a little more careful than I do, though he's the most daring man in the world. Six weeks of marriage teaches you an awful lot about a man. But our marriage, Malcolm, will just last on and on, precious . . ."

Leaning over the table, she kissed him a long time now on the lips. "Breath like a haymow!" she pointed out.

She shook her head, tears standing in her eyes again.

"I think Brownie should announce the engagement and/or marriage," she said *sotto voce* to Malcolm. "I have some more numbers to sing tonight, you know."

A trio had taken the place of Melba as she was talking to Malcolm and Gus, but a signal had been just given that she was to resume her part of the program.

"I think just a short announcement of our engagement is in order," Melba said to Gus.

"Darling, you do love me, and you want to marry me—before they announce our betrothal over the loudspeaker?" Melba said anxiously to Malcolm.

"Melba, *yes*!" the boy said.

"Oh, Brownie"—Melba turned to Gus—"I'll never forget you for having brought Malcolm to me, dearest. Don't ever let me forget this great favor you have committed for me . . ."

When Gus, however, did not get up from the table to announce the engagement, Melba became very upset again.

"Did you not hear me tell you?" she commanded the motor-cyclist. "You are to announce our engagement and/or marriage. Kindly do so at once. The trio has played its last number minutes ago . . . I'm nearly ready to go on!"

Gus got up slowly, opened his leather riding jacket, from under which a handsome watch chain of the last century was suspended, and cleared his throat; his immense rich voice informed the entire room of contemporaries of the coming marriage of Malcolm and Melba.

"On Tuesday next!" Melba, standing up, informed the room.

Owing to his having drunk perhaps more than was his custom, or perhaps because he had stood so long on his feet in the horticultural gardens, Malcolm had some special difficulty in getting up, but with Melba and Gus's assistance, he finally did rise and acknowledge the applause and recognition of the audience. After which he and Melba kissed one another in front of everybody.

"This is to be a serious and lifelong affair," Melba informed people, tears again in her eyes.

Malcolm then sat down again at the table with Gus, while Melba went up to the stage microphone and sang again her three numbers, including the one which, Gus explained, had made her internationally famous:

> *Hot in the rocker,*
> *But so cool on the grain—!*

At the end of her last number, Melba hastened, after only a perfunctory acknowledgment of applause (so rare to her), to Malcolm and Gus's table, where she kissed the boy passionately, but with perhaps a slight bit more restraint.

"My only one," she explained to Malcolm, and she handed him a roll of bills, "now that our marriage is a fact which only time will make final, I want things to be all up and above board. We could so easily consummate everything there is to consummate here and now, as Brownie and I once did so long ago, and Freddie, too, but as I told the contemporaries a few minutes ago, I want this marriage to last. It's to be the real thing, Malcolm, precious," and here she placed a napkin to her eyes. "I've got the real thing is all, Brownie." She turned weeping to the motorcyclist. "Lightning, that's all you can say about it."

When she had got control of her voice, she went on:

"Brownie will take care of you. He'll be like a father to you . . . Don't interrupt me!" she warned Malcolm when the latter made vociferous sounds of interpolation. "I have to sing another number in a minute, owing to that mammoth applause I am getting, and I just wanted to say that I want Gus here to take awful good care of you. Tuesday will be here before we know it, but we mustn't meet again till then . . ."

Kissing Malcolm again on the mouth for the last time, Melba turned briefly to Gus, to whom she handed a small fat package of something, and whispered:

"Mature him up just a little while you're gone," and without another word or nod to either of them, she made her way to a small door marked AUTHORITY, and opening it, disappeared.

The Tattoo Palace

"How the A-all am I goin' to mature you up by Tuesday?" Gus inquired of Malcolm, as the two rode off again together on the motorcycle, this time in the direction back to the city. "You motherless bastard," Gus complained, turning his head around.

"My father is the one who is missing!" Malcolm shouted to Gus through the wind, but Gus did not let on he had heard a thing from him.

"Do you know the honor you have all just received?" Gus inquired, turning his head back to Malcolm. "Marriage with *her*."

"I think I do," Malcolm shouted into Gus's ear.

"She's the greatest now, and will be the greatest then," Gus said.

In their heated conversation Gus had forgotten to stop at the private contemporary gas pump to refill his tank and, as a result of this oversight, near the edge of the city his motorcycle stopped, out of fuel.

"That's what distraction will do for you," Gus complained peevishly. "Hop down, and let's go hunt for a pump."

They walked slowly together toward the pink glow of the city.

"We got only till Tuesday, mind," Gus kept repeating. "Only till Tuesday."

"Will it be a big wedding, sir?" Malcolm inquired.

Gus paused, staring at him.

"What you call me *sir* for if you a contemporary? Is that a *code* word you picked up in some other society?"

Gus stopped dead in his tracks. "What you call me that for, Malcolm?" He relented a little when he had studied the boy's face.

"Just for the usual," Malcolm explained, fancying his speech now did sound like that of a contemporary.

"Then *don't*!" Gus warned him. "Don't *sir* me."

And then without another word Gus sat down on the curb and began making sounds which resembled sobbing a great deal.

"I can't give up that damned bitch!" he said.

"Who?" Malcolm comforted him, putting his hand on Gus's sleeve.

"Who, he asks me who?" and Gus's voice broke again into falsetto.

"He asks me who." Gus shook his head, seeming to be talking to his shoes. "Melba's in my blood," he sighed. "It's like that awful kind of malaria they can't do nothing for you with . . ."

Gus began to quiet down then a little. Then, getting up slowly, he said:

"Come on, Malco, we got to go through with this. I would cut off my right arm right up to here for her, but I will make you her husband or bust in the attempt . . . You keep full confidence in me now."

Malcolm nodded.

After they had walked a few more blocks, Gus said he had to rest again, as he was not a walker, and they sat down on the curb.

"Look at all this money Melba give me to mature you up

with," Gus said, pulling out a roll of bills from his pocket. "That one bill curlin' around my thumb there is a thousand dollar one."

Malcolm glanced briefly at the bill.

"You not impressed," the motorcyclist said. "I hope this wedding ain't goin' to waste on you."

Down the street a little way, its many-colored lights moving and gesticulating like a brightly lit kaleidoscope, shone a sign with the words:

ROBINOLTE'S TATTOO PALACE

Malcolm read off the words.

"That's the place now to be matured," Gus said, ironical.

Malcolm exclaimed: "My father had a tattoo, and he often said to me"—and in his excitement the boy spit on Gus's face, for which he immediately apologized—"my father said to me, 'One day you must be tattooed, son.' "

Gus looked off, disgust and weariness on his face.

"Are you tattooed, by any chance?" Malcolm inquired, more to punctuate the depressing silence than to have his question answered.

Gus looked at him with pity.

"I been admired by women all my life for my chest and arms, and my body in general," Gus began. "Why have them chopped up by needles, or *dis*-jointed by designs?"

"But one or two tattoos for a wedding is surely . . . well, *usual*," Malcolm brought out, swallowing hard, and wondering at the same time where he had ever heard what he had just said.

Gus replied immediately: "But I BEEN married! Three times!"

"Get tattooed with me," Malcolm said, unaware again what prompted him to say these words.

"Do you know what you are?" Gus inquired, a strange equanimity and warmth coming over him. "Persuasive, that's what."

"You agree, then?" Malcolm cried, his enthusiasm mounting.

"If we should get tattoos," Gus began, opening his jacket and taking out his nineteenth-century watch for a look at the hour, "if we have the tattoos, we must have the real ones, you know: the spread-eagle one on the chest, especially. The rest don't really count. Real men have to have the chest tattoos or nothing."

"My father—" Malcolm began, but Gus put his hand over the boy's mouth.

"I got the floor, kiddy," Gus went on. "Now you don't need the peter tattoo, say," he explained in his deepest voice, "on account of Tuesday, but we could easy get fixed up for all the rest."

"Hurray!" Malcolm clapped his hands together.

"You a *brave* boy?" Gus asked him, and he smiled for the first time at Malcolm, and his ivory teeth flashed in the dark between them.

"As I say," Gus went on, "I done been there before, and I know Professor Robinolte, the tattoo king, but before, you com-*pre*-hend, I only was to *watch*."

"I suppose it is bloody," the boy ventured.

Gus thought for a moment. "I didn't see much *blood* . . . More the sight of white lips and occasional screams." He laughed. "A few fainted that day. Mostly sailors."

"Well, I should be more scared, but somehow I'm not," Malcolm told Gus.

He yawned. "For one thing," the boy said, "I'm too sleepy to be scared."

Gus studied Malcolm. "I wish *I* could be sleepy," he said. "I been *wide*-awake all my life, and I need some rest. I could take a long long rest."

"Should we have a drink before we go?" Malcolm wondered.

"No," Gus answered. "I think a man has got to simply surrender to them needles and the pain."

"I always thought that . . . Abyssinians were braver than other people," Malcolm said, bringing his face closer to that of the motorcyclist's.

"A-byss—!!" and here Gus broke off into a snort and a laugh. "You do me up," he said after a moment.

"But why fear a little needle?" Malcolm wondered, perhaps to himself.

"You wait and see," Gus told him. "I been everywhere. One war and then Korea . . . But when it comes to lie still and be dotted on by the old tattoo man, that's a kind of bravery I do not got. But we got to mature you, like she say, that's the thing . . . And you know what I think of Melba, not to mention what I owe her . . ."

Gus stood up and pushed out his chest, perhaps already feeling the beginning of the tattoo professor's art upon him.

"Say, how about you," Gus finally said. "You TERRIBLE young, it seems to me, to be *de*-corated."

"I'm not so young now any more," Malcolm told him, still sitting on the curb. "And it will be a change, you see. I like a certain amount of change. The only thing about a tattoo is, once it's done, I don't suppose you can undo it away again."

"That's so," Gus said. "But you was the one asked now, hear?"

The Tattoo Palace was both severe and cosy—severe because it bore every witness to the painful operations enacted within —the electrical tattooing needles, the bloody rags, the bottles of disinfectant and smelling salts, and the bloodstains on the floor; cosy because Professor Robinolte himself, the tattoo artist, was a pleasant blond young man who exhibited four front gold teeth, and cared for all his customers like members of his family, sending them annual birthday and Christmas greetings, and often advising them on their domestic and professional careers, while somewhere behind him soft music poured forth, and the air itself was sprayed with moderately expensive *eau de cologne.*

However, an air of terrible expectancy weighted the atmosphere.

The password to allow anyone to enter Professor Robinolte's *boutique* was a secret one, which Gus now whispered in the professor's ear.

"Meet Melba's husband-to-be." Gus next pointed Malcolm out to Professor Robinolte.

"Not again so soon," Professor Robinolte cried, but nevertheless congratulated Malcolm. "I used to think that Melba was young," the professor said, taking a better look at Malcolm. "But this one—!!"

"How about decorating the bridegroom up a bit." Gus got down to brass tacks. "Melba would like him a few months older anyhow."

"You know the law, Brownie." Professor Robinolte was a bit coy.

"Don't give me no law talk now," Gus said wearily, and he sat down on an ice-cream chair.

"I'll tell you what, Brownie." Professor Robinolte toyed with the largest of his electrical needles, and blew something off the tip of it. "I'll tattoo the kid if I can tattoo you in the bargain."

"There we go again!" Gus shook his head. "What I ain't done for Melba."

"I've never got a real good tattoo on anybody with your special color skin." Professor Robinolte complimented the motorcyclist in strictly professional tones. "I'm so tired of pink and tan skins."

Gus spat on the floor.

"All right," the motorcyclist began, "I won't chicken on either Melba or her here-bridegroom." And he peeled off his leather jacket and would have taken off the shirt beneath it, had Professor Robinolte not halted him with a gesture.

"Grooms first, please," the professor said. Then: "Remember when *you* were Melba's husband, Brownie?"

Gus made a significant sound with his lips at the professor, and moved his ice-cream chair back out of the main arena.

"As far as I'm concerned—did you say your name was Malcolm?" the professor began. "As far as I'm concerned—in case we should both of us ever be before the police and the courts —you are all of eighteen years old tonight . . . Is that clear?"

The thought of being eighteen years old was pleasing to

Malcolm, and he agreed now that he was. Eighteen, unlike fifteen, was full of promise and adventure.

At a signal from the professor, Gus assisted the latter, and in the twinkling of an eye, lifted Malcolm up and put him in a kind of reclining chair, and removed all of his clothes, depositing these in a basket behind them.

The professor quickly traced on Malcolm's chest the outlines of a black leopard, which was the design Gus had, after a moment's study, chosen for the boy.

Malcolm laughed a good deal while the tracing was done, so close to his nipples, and Gus turned a peculiar shade of indeterminate color while watching.

When the actual work with the needle began, with its accompanying bouncing ominous sound, Malcolm looked more grave, but at the same time amused.

"Don't you feel anything?" Gus asked Malcolm several times, when the professor would stop momentarily to spunge off the blood from where it had obscured the design.

Malcolm shook his head. The professor exchanged looks with Gus.

After the long but highly successful session of putting the black panther on Malcolm's chest, during which Malcolm seemed to have dozed off, Professor Robinolte shook the boy and asked him if he was prepared to have the carnations placed above his right biceps, and the daggers on his forearms.

Malcolm said he was, and these designs were perpetrated, too.

The entire difficulty came with Gus, who, of course, later felt very small and ashamed.

While stretched out on the same chair, submitting to the black panther tattoo on his chest, Gus fainted three times, but always insisted on the tattooing being resumed again—over Professor Robinolte's protests. However, only one carnation was given the motorcyclist, and the professor was pleased, at the end of the operation, at the triumph of color on Brownie's chest, despite the countless difficulties which beset them.

Gus blamed his faintheartedness on his concern for Malcolm,

and on his having first watched the savage needles at work on so young a man.

But Professor Robinolte told him brutally and often that Gus was simply not the type who could be tattooed, his two war records notwithstanding.

Bandaged and dressed again, the two men stood taking their leave of Professor Robinolte who—after promising to send them birthday greetings and Christmas cards for the rest of their lives—warned them not to use water on their fresh tattoos, not to expose the tattoos to the unprotected sun, and above all, take it easy and not touch or scratch the wounds.

Professor Robinolte then complimented Malcolm on his amazing bravery, which, he said, he had never quite encountered before, and congratulated him on his coming marriage to Melba.

"You could hardly be in more competent hands," Professor Robinolte told him, though a certain air of dubiety and concern crossed and recrossed his face.

"You will be the pride of all women and some men, to half-quote somebody," the professor called to them, as they left his *boutique,* and Gus and Malcolm walked off toward the center of town.

"And good luck!" Professor Robinolte shouted. "Christ knows, you need it," he said in lower tones to himself.

At Madame Rosita's

They walked slower and slower toward the city, owing to the fact, as Gus explained again, he had been a motorcyclist too long to know how to walk, and he didn't actually like to be seen walking any more, it kind of hurt his self-respect, and another reason, he would not deny it, he was a bit knocked off by those electric needles of Professor Robinolte.

Clearing his throat and putting his arm around Malcolm, then, in tones of fatherly intimacy, Gus said, "Kiddy, I didn't bring you out here for you just to have your hide embroidered. I got to ask you a plain question now on account of there is Tuesday."

Malcolm nodded, smiling.

"To put it delicate-like, Malco"—Gus stopped now in his tracks—"have you ever been completely and solidly joined to a woman?"

"Well," Malcolm remembered, "in a brief kind of way."

"Brief, huh?" Gus said, snorting. "Now see here," but just then a twinge of pain in his chest made him stop for a moment. "See here now . . . On account of who you are marrying, kiddy, you got to be ready . . . An old tattoo ain't any number-one preparation. If anything it may make you too sore to *be* a good groom. No, Malco, what I am talking about is good old solid Nature. Have you been joined to a woman the way Nature meant? Yes or no."

Malcolm opened his mouth, but it closed immediately again.

"I can see you ain't," Gus said. "Well, that's what Melba sent us out for, to mature you up."

Gus then pointed with his arm to a large house in the near distance.

"Do you see that house over there?" he asked. "That's where I'm going to take you. Rosita's. Madame Rosita's, they used to call her. You heard of her?"

Malcolm shook his head.

"You ain't heard of *any*-thing," Gus complained, and then he said well, that was what he was for, et cetera.

They went up to the house, before which was a sign that read:

PRIVATE AND TURKISH BATHS
CABINETS AND OVER-NIGHT COTTAGES
$2.00

They went down a flight of stairs, and Gus rapped lightly on a small wooden partition, which immediately opened, and a man with a green visor looked out.

"Gus, is that really you!" the man said. Then, looking at Malcolm, he exclaimed: "Where did you find *him*?"

"A Turkish bath for me, and a room upstairs for the boy here," Gus explained.

The man was about to say something, perhaps in protest, when Gus handed him part of the roll of bills which Melba had given him.

"I was just wondering, Gus," the attendant said obsequiously, "if you had observed that that boy has blood stains on him."

"They just tattooed him," Gus retorted.

"This way," the man replied, coughing nervously, ushering

them into a waiting room down which tall coat-hangers were lined like trees, and off each coat-hanger was the door to a room.

Gus, turning to Malcolm, said, "Now downstairs here, kiddy, is the Turkish bath department, and upstairs is where you are going to go. When you through, come down here and wake me. Which is my room, Miles?" he addressed the attendant.

"You pick one out. Nobody here tonight at all," Miles replied.

"All right now." Gus fumbled about, almost as if he had lost his sense of balance, and then looking straight ahead of him, almost blindly, he said: "What number is this now . . ."

"Twenty-two," Miles said.

"That will be me, then," Gus told Malcolm. "I'm twenty-two."

Just then a woman of indeterminate age, with purple markings beneath and on her eyelids, entered, bringing with her the mixed perfumes of, say, bay rum (domestic), and lily of the valley.

"Brownie, darling, it's been *years*!" the woman cried, and she hit him playfully with her fist on his chest.

Gus bent double under the blow, coughing loudly.

"It's Professor Robinolte's needles," Malcolm explained to the woman, who was staring at Gus with a puzzled twist of a smile on her lips.

"Fine shape you're in to come to see me," she said, after a pause of uncomprehension.

Gus resumed his normal standing position again, and whispered, "It's the boy this time . . . I'm just going to take a brief shower and a snooze . . . Ain't had no sleep in a week, you know . . ."

"Let me get this all down," the woman said. "You're sending *him*" she pointed to Malcolm "upstairs for *you*."

"Break him in, for Christ's sakes, will you?" Gus said, coughing wearily, and he sat down on a chair near his coat-hanger, and began taking off his shoes.

"You do like I told you now, back in the street," Gus admonished the boy. "I want you to go through it all just like I told you Nature meant."

The woman made a contemptuous sound with her lips at Gus.

"Come on with me, honey," the woman then told Malcolm, and giving Gus a last severe look, she and Malcolm started off together without another word.

"And don't come back without you had it," Gus managed to shout at Malcolm. He coughed very loud, and then he tried to say something else, but the words could not be heard.

Four or five hours had passed when Malcolm tiptoed back to Room Number 22 of the Turkish bath section, rapped, then when there was no answer, opened the door softly, and peeked in.

Gus lay on a small cot, unclothed now except for his tattoo bandages, which were, however, nearly coming off.

Malcolm sat down on a small white chair which was next to the cot.

"I did just like you said, Gus," he told the motorcyclist. "All the way through three times! So it looks like I'll be a bridegroom after all."

Malcolm thought that Gus smiled, and he was pleased.

"Don't you think we should be getting back to our motorcycle now?" Malcolm inquired.

The rays of the morning sun were pouring in from a tiny window above Gus's cot.

"Time to get up." Malcolm yawned enormously, and he tapped Gus gently, being careful to choose a place that was not tattooed.

Malcolm went on talking, meanwhile, about how Madame Rosita herself had complimented him, and given him tea, and presented him with a little keepsake, namely an old-fashioned shaving mug with a picture of George Washington and the first American flag, which he now showed to Gus.

But Gus slept on.

Blood had hardened and caked through the bandages over

his chest. Looking a little more closely at his abdomen, Malcolm started a bit, for he thought he could observe no rise and fall of that part of his friend. Malcolm looked at his mouth, too, which was strangely drawn and silent.

"Gus," he said rather loudly. "Brownie! *Morning*!"

Malcolm drew out a small piece of paper from his pocket, and put it in front of Gus's mouth and nose, for his father had always told him that this was the sure way of determining whether a person was alive or dead. But nothing came out from the motorcyclist to stir the paper.

"Gus," he shouted now, and he put his hand on the dark man's forehead and on the tight black curls of his head.

"Gus," he said, feeling the cold of the man's body, "—*you're* dead!"

Hurrying to tell the attendant, Malcolm dropped his new gift of the shaving mug, which broke into twenty or thirty small colored pieces on the floor.

He had some difficulty in arousing the attendant, and when the attendant did come out from his small cubicle, he was not the one who had been called Miles at all, of the night before.

"Gus is dead in Room Number Twenty-Two!" Malcolm cried.

"Who ain't at this hour?" the man replied gruffly and suspiciously.

Malcolm took hold of the attendant's arm, urging him to come.

"Look, Lord Fauntleroy," the man said. "Get out of here before there's any trouble. You're too goddamn young to be in here in the first place. Who let you in?"

"Gus . . . the dead man!" Malcolm cried.

Coming clear out from his cubicle, the man took hold of Malcolm and ushered him to the front door.

"Now get out," he ordered, kicking the boy, and he slammed the door on him, after giving him a further kick.

"Get out and stay out!"

Malcolm stood, however, outside the door, knocking and

gesticulating in the direction of Room Number 22.

"It's Gus," he cried to the attendant, who had already disappeared back into his cubicle. "Gus, the motorcyclist! Can't you understand?"

For the first time since his father's disappearance, Malcolm shed not just a few but a torrent of tears. He cried all the way back to the edge of the town, a flood of weeping which he had never thought could possibly come from a human being. He no longer felt he was a man at all, as he had at Madame Rosita's, and at times he whimpered like a five-year-old child.

He stopped near a telephone pole, on which there was a picture of Melba before a microphone, and a caption under the picture, AMERICA'S NUMBER ONE CHANTEUSE, and vomited for a few minutes.

Then wiping his mouth and his eyes, with a handkerchief which he believed Gus himself must have given him, he carefully kissed the picture of Melba on the telephone pole. "So long, lovely," he said.

It never occurred to him then, in his despair, that he would ever find Melba again, and the thought of marriage was as remote as any other thing in his past, his father's voice, or the bench.

All he knew he could do was keep walking.

Melba's marriage

Malcolm's adventures might have been continued indefinitely had it not so happened by chance, days later, that Melba, driving in her second ex-husband's Daimler, stopped at a roadside drugstore for cigarettes and mascara, when she caught sight of her husband-to-be at the soda fountain spooning up the last of a strawberry soda, while telling the clerk, who seemed to hang helplessly on his words, what was an involved story.

"Precious!" Melba cried in stentorian tones.

Everyone in the drugstore recognized that voice. Before Melba could take another step toward Malcolm, she was surrounded by admirers and autograph-seekers, who demanded her signature on matchboxes, hot-dog wrappers, and soda-fountain straws, while a gasoline attendant asked her to write her name with lipstick on his forehead, which she immediately did.

"Gus is dead, Brownie is dead!" Malcolm cried, having got off the stool to the soda fountain, but unable to advance toward Melba owing to her crowd of admirers.

Melba nodded, meaning, it seemed, she knew all about Gus.

When the crowd had once dispersed a little, Melba went up to Malcolm and kissed him quietly. Someone flashed a bulb from a camera.

Back in the front seat of her car, the leather being so badly torn it was difficult to sit still in comfort, Melba explained to Malcolm the trouble she was having with her Hollywood manager.

Melba knew all about Brownie or Gus's death, and would not talk about it for a good stretch. Then turning her attention to Gus briefly, she said: "But haven't you seen the newspapers, for crying out loud? I had to attend the damned inquest . . ."

Before Malcolm could say more, Melba had kissed him fifteen or sixteen successive times on the mouth.

"Oh, angel, is it ever good to see you," she said. "Another five minutes, and I would have *never* found you. I would have ended up marrying someone else . . . sure as fate."

Pulling open a compartment in the car, Melba then brought out a packet of letters.

"From your friend Madame Girard," Melba said. "She's trying to prevent us getting married."

"You know Madame Girard!" Malcolm exclaimed.

"I know everybody," Melba said, rather severely, and Malcolm suddenly felt the gulf which separated him from fame. After all, of course, everybody knew Melba, even if she didn't know everybody, and she was as famous in Japan and India as she was in Paris and Chicago.

"Now how about that wedding," Melba said, starting the motor. "Tuesday, you know, came and went in a *big* hurry. But I got the license, with a little bomb or two at city hall, and I got the justice of the peace under wraps. All we have to do is appear. How about this PM?"

Malcolm cried yes, and bent over to kiss Melba, but she said not while she was driving, and that she had spent one year in a California hospital for kissing a marine while driving.

Malcolm then mentioned Gus again, and Melba was again severe.

"Don't give Brownie another thought, if you value my time

and my love. For one thing, he was jealous of you, anyhow. But for Christ's sake, it was his time to go and all, good grief. He'd had it, and it was his time."

"His tattoos didn't kill him?"

"Tattoos, your mother. Why, Brownie had been half-dead for years. Most of his guts were blown out in Korea. Still, he kept on going. And on what? God knows. Don't give him a thought, precious. He was sweet, and of course I married him at one time, but it was his *time* to go," she said, narrowly missing a curve, "and there just isn't anything to be sorry about. When it's your time, well, it is.

"We'll be terribly happy together," Melba went on. "But you'll have to give up this Madame Girard woman, though Christ knows why she's called that, and whatever she may have meant to you. She's *dangerous*!"

"But what about Girard Girard?" Malcolm exclaimed.

"Oh, why ever even *think* about him." Melba was firm.

Both Madame Girard and Girard Girard made several attempts to communicate with Malcolm. Girard Girard himself wrote a letter on embossed stationery so thick that it had burst through the envelope, and part of it was lost, in which he explained the reason for his having failed to keep his appointment with Malcolm in the horticultural gardens. Melba did not show this communication to Malcolm.

Malcolm and Melba were married in Chicago, after a good deal of difficulty owing to Malcolm's lack of a birth certificate, and his general appearance. After the ceremony had taken place, they flew to the Caribbean, as Melba said she loved to be in countries where everything was blowing up, and the USA was much too quiet for her in any case. Also, she wanted to meet some of the new Cuban musicians, who put us all so to shame.

After a week in Cuba, however, Melba grew homesick for her country house, which, as yet, Malcolm had never even seen, and as Malcolm, too, was nostalgic for the environs of those places where he had had his bench, and had met Mr. Cox, Kermit, Estel Blanc, and the Girards—although all of these persons Melba had forbidden Malcolm ever to see or communicate with again—the couple returned to begin their matrimonial career.

Madame Girard telephoned four or five times daily, and as Melba was nearly always gone, Malcolm welcomed these communications from his old life, although Madame Girard was drinking so heavily, she seldom told him much, or actually said much herself.

Malcolm told Madame Girard that he liked marriage very much, though it took a great deal out of him. He hoped that Madame Girard would come soon, to visit, and he told her about his new tattoos.

Melba had brought back a young Cuban man to be Malcolm's personal valet, but as the latter spoke very little English, Malcolm's only verbal communication with the outside world was largely on the telephone with the weather-report operator and, when she was sober enough to know that she was talking with him, Madame Girard.

Madame Girard finally broke the news to Malcolm that Girard Girard had secured a divorce from her and finally married Laureen Raphaelson, and that Laureen was already pregnant.

"Marriage for him," Madame Girard explained, "was not emotion, but to produce an heir to his fortune."

About the fourth month of Malcolm's marriage, the Cuban valet pointed out to Melba that her young husband was losing weight, but the singer was quick to assure the Cuban that he must remember American men did not weigh so much as the easier-going Latin peoples, and the subject was not brought up again.

Melba was extremely busy that fall and winter, and seldom came home except to sleep when, as she said later, every joy of marriage was tasted, though rapidly, to the full.

A strange thing did happen, she remembered later, long, long after Malcolm's time. It was on one of her few free evenings, and she and her young husband had gone to a well-known night club.

As usual now, Malcolm drank a great deal too much, and talked a good deal more about his father, Mr. Cox, and Kermit, and Melba complained, as she now did more frequently, that the more she heard Malcolm talk the less she realized they had in common, except, as she was hasty to add, *that one thing, dear,* and after all, she added, what is marriage based on but that.

"I didn't marry you for your mind," Melba always said, "and you do get better-looking every day. I like you thin, but I suppose I would like you fat, too. And though you're not exactly the type I would spot on the street, once I've come to be with you, you're the only one out of a large assortment."

She kissed Malcolm several times. She had had her hair tinted a different shade for this evening and was wearing special immense dark glasses designed specially for her, so that she could pretend nobody recognized her, and could let herself go a little bit more.

Malcolm kept excusing himself to go to the men's room, which always annoyed her, and yet these little breaks from his talk were not unwelcome.

"You're annoying, kiddy," Melba said, "but you make up for the whole crumby thing back at the house."

Their drinks that evening were the usual rum sours, with a dash of something special Melba always carried with her, she didn't tell Malcolm what.

It was after their tenth or twelfth rum sour with Melba's own little special recipe thrown in that Malcolm cried out in the loudest voice she had ever heard him use—the voice almost of a man now:

"That's HE—my FATHER!"

Melba tried to restrain him, but he got up quickly from his table and went in the direction of a middle-aged unemphatically distinguished man, who might have posed for sparkling water advertisements.

The man went into the lavatory, and Malcolm followed.

"Father!" Malcolm cried, stretching out his arms to the man, who was washing his hands gingerly in a deep bowl of water. "Where did you *go* all this time?"

The man looked up briefly, unflustered and calm. Having washed his hands, he examined his mustache closely in the mirror.

"Don't you recognize me?" Malcolm cried to him. "I would recognize *you* anywhere!"

The man now opened his mouth and examined his teeth carefully, touching the front two teeth to remove, perhaps, a particle therefrom.

Going up close to the man, Malcolm touched him gently on his shoulder.

"If you will only allow me, sir, I can identify you . . . By the small bullet hole you carry beneath your collar bone."

"Would you allow me to pass," the man told Malcolm, and he made an effort, aiming at equanimity, to go out.

"You are pretending not to recognize me, sir!" Malcolm cried. "Is it because I married Melba, or because I left the bench?"

"Allow me to pass," the man said, greatly disturbed.

"If you will not allow me to recognize you, let me show you your own identification mark. Remember, Father, you always told me that if any questions were ever asked in a fatal emergency, you could be identified by this small gunshot wound which you suffered in the armed forces."

Grasping the man, then, by his collar, Malcolm attempted to undo his shirt in the hope that the exposure of the bullet wound would prove beyond cavil that he was his father and that Malcolm was his son.

Becoming now seriously alarmed, the man cried for assistance, which only led to Malcolm's seizing his "father" more securely, while the latter, now panic-stricken and feeling Malcolm seize him not only about his chest, but also securely about his leg, in a sudden paroxysm of anger and terror, knocked the boy heavily to the marble floor, just as a policeman entered the room.

"Arrest that pederast!" the man said to the officer. "He attacked me!"

"Sir," Malcolm cried, addressing perhaps his "father" and the police officer together, "oh, sir, I am NOT Mr. Cox . . . I am MALCOLM!"

The "father," seeing perhaps now that Malcolm was indeed too young to be anything, snorted, wheeled, and walking out of the lavatory, disappeared into the inner recesses of the night club.

But what was Malcolm's relief and joy when, looking more closely at the policeman from his position on the floor, he saw that the officer was the very same man into whose arms he had rushed that evening long ago on the occasion of his visit to Estel Blanc's.

The police officer, who had recognized Malcolm even more promptly than the boy had recognized him, helped him up from the floor.

"Again I find you in suspicious surroundings, although older," the officer said, and he examined the bump on the boy's scalp.

The officer shook his head seriously, ignoring the babble of *thankyou sir*s, et cetera, which came from Malcolm's lips.

"What did that gentleman call you?" the officer wondered.

"My father?"

The policeman gazed wonderingly at Malcolm.

"Why, a pederast," Malcolm answered the policeman's question.

"Are you one, sir?" the officer asked in a thin grave voice.

"Why, I don't believe I'm old enough, am I?" Malcolm replied.

The officer folded his arms, thinking.

"You have to study the stars a good deal to be one, you know," Malcolm added for the policeman's information. "Mr. Cox, the astrologer, would be able to tell you."

The policeman's jaw moved slightly up and out, but as he did not say anything, Malcolm continued:

"Would you care to meet my wife, sir?"

"You've gone and got married, in the bargain?" the officer exclaimed.

"Yes," Malcolm admitted, a bit shamefaced, "though I had to tell the marriage bureau I was eighteen. But do please come and meet Melba. She's awfully famous."

The policeman pinched off some lint which had become attached to his handsome uniform, and then told Malcolm that he would not be able to accept his invitation but how pleasant, actually, it had been running into him again after all this passage of time. He then shook hands with the boy, and as a last gesture, patted Malcolm rather soberly on the shoulder:

"Always behave like a man, Malcolm, and you'll have nothing to regret."

Just as the boy was about to leave, the officer, struggling and reluctant, but earnest, called him back again, and clearing his throat loudly, said:

"If I were you, Malcolm, I believe I would look up that word the man you called your 'father' used about you in this lavatory. I don't think you know what a good many words mean, as I recall our interview of some time past, in the station—probably all owing to you not having gone to school enough."

"I see." Malcolm considered this advice. "But I don't know, sir, whether I will have the time to look the word up or not, you see. I'm awfully busy now that I'm married."

"You *take* the time, Malco," the policeman said. "And now run on back to your *wife*."

"Thank you, sir, and good luck, sir!"

When Malcolm had gone, the police officer went over to the same washbasin which the "father" had employed, removed his smart hat, and then quickly lowering his head, allowed water to trickle over his scalp and forehead.

"My father refused to recognize me," Malcolm told Melba when he had returned to her table.

Melba looked glassily at him. She had drunk a good many of her special concoctions while he had been gone.

"Look, kiddy," Melba said. "I've been meaning to give you this speech, but the long and the short of it is: grow up a little.

That wasn't your father. I've known that old pot since I was ten. He's nobody's father. And what's this *idée* unfix about your father. Who wants a father? It's been old hat for years. That old pot, I repeat, was nobody's father."

"But he looked like him to a T," Malcolm insisted, rubbing the bump on his scalp.

"Millions of men look like millions of men, especially Americans," Melba said, beginning on a new drink the waiter had just brought her. "In fact, most men look like most men. That's why I go for you, kiddy. You're unique all over."

She kissed Malcolm wetly on both his eyes, and he flushed with excitement.

"He wasn't my father?" Malcolm inquired from her after a while, and he shifted in his seat several times.

"With my fame and money," Melba told him, "and your special gift, blow your father," and she motioned for him to sip her drink.

"Blow my father!" Malcolm echoed, and then hearing his own voice, his jaw dropped loosely.

"Say, kiddy, are you all right?" Melba said, somewhat concerned.

"Blow my father!" Malcolm said.

"Don't say that again," Melba adjured him, and her mouth set.

Malcolm stared in the direction of, but not focusing on, Melba.

Looking at her bridegroom a bit more closely, she asked: "Say, kiddy, who gave you that knock on the head? And you got a real shiner coming!"

"Blow my fath—" Malcolm began, and then put his hand to his mouth to show he should not say that.

Melba put her fingers to the boy's scalp, and bringing her hand down, saw it smeared with the well-known fluid, as she called it, which at her touch had begun trickling down his forehead and face, like a rivulet in spring.

Melba quickly staunched the flow with a napkin she took from the empty table next to them.

"Have a drink, kiddy," she said. "It's wonderful for cuts and bruises and abrasions of all kinds."

"Maybe my father never existed," Malcolm said, and his tones were now like those of Melba's.

"Who the hell knows if anybody ever existed?" she said, but her old gay manner was missing. "You relax now, kiddy. Forget what happened in that lavatory, and drink up. Last call for alcohol, like they say. Drink up."

"It's *not* twenty years!"

~~~~~~

When Malcolm woke up the next afternoon, his hair, except for where the blood had dyed it a startling crimson, was snow white, *whiter* indeed, as he remarked to Melba, in bed, than he had ever remembered his father's being.

"You look simply grand," Melba said, "not to mention it's a miracle of some dumb kind. Jesus, are you beautiful. I want to just stay in bed and look at you. Jesus, white hair, kiddy."

"I am O.K., then, Melba, girl?" Malcolm wondered, and his voice again did not quite sound like his own.

"You ain't never been better, kiddy," Melba assured him. "Let Mama kiss her white-haired angel boy."

Melba kissed him on his new hair.

Then loosening Malcolm's pajama tops, she began kissing him on the chest.

He tried to return the compliment by kissing her hair, but his head hurt too much when he moved it.

"Your white hair goes so good with your pink skin," Melba remarked. "It makes you look both dark and light."

"Melba, honey, ring for the coffee. I'm awful excited over

you like always, but I seem too dizzy to make love."

"I'll ring for the coffee," Melba said, still entranced. "And I'll make all the love today. Don't talk about making love. What did I buy you for, kiddy?"

She kissed his chest again.

"Answer me that," she said. "What did I buy you for?"

"You bought me?" Malcolm groaned a bit, under her caresses.

"Down payment, lock, stock, and barrel," Melba replied, leaving a watery kiss behind. "Mmm. Talk about plums for texture. And with white hair!"

Drinking her coffee later, she walked up and down the room, occasionally darting a glance at Malcolm, who remained quiet and still in bed. Practicing her new repertoire, she sang one of her favorite songs especially now for Malcolm:

> *I'm a little bit of this and that,*
> *But I'm all one solid piece for you!*

Malcolm smiled, weak but appreciative, from the bed.

If there is one thing that is fatal to most men, Mr. Cox always told his followers, it is marriage. Malcolm was not precisely a full-grown man, but he was a man, and marriage in his case may have proved fatal.

Not one of the circle surrounding Madame Girard and Mr. Cox had ever thought that Malcolm, who had been with them such a short time, would go from them in the particular way he did. But after it was all over, everybody agreed that it was almost the only way he could have gone from them.

Too young for the army, too unprepared to continue his schooling and become a scientist, too untrained for ordinary work—what was left for him but marriage? And in his case, marriage supplied him with everything that he had up to now lacked, and also gave him his unique way of leaving the world, in which he had perhaps never belonged (as some people said) in the first place.

Marriage, which ushers most people into life, in Malcolm's case, therefore, ushered him into happiness—and death.

Whether Melba sensed that Malcolm was dying, no one ever knew. She was too busy ever to talk with anybody, and besides, she did not know Madame Girard and Mr. Cox and their circle, and they were the only ones who would have been able to tell her what state Malcolm was in.

Melba's chief source of interest during this period was that after so many weeks of incessant marriage, she found she was still not pregnant, and could therefore continue both her professional career and her marriage duties to Malcolm without fear or constraint, and what is more, they could, husband and wife, go their separate ways quite freely, as before marriage.

Since the night he had recognized his "father" and cut open his head, Malcolm found himself too weak ever to be out of bed, and in this state the happy thought hit him to write down all his conversations with Mr. Cox, Girard Girard, Kermit, and others in English, but shortly after he began this, he caught an extremely bad cold, which his Cuban valet said was really pneumonia, and after that, Malcolm wrote down everything in French, as this seemed the easier language in his increased weakness.

Melba knew French very well, but, as she explained, since she had begun to read his "conversations" in English, she lost all the little interest she had had in them once he switched to another language, and so nobody ever saw them again until Malcolm himself was no longer counted among the living.

As Malcolm felt his strength ebbing rather than returning, a fixed melancholy stole over him, and the sight of the falling leaves and November skies fixed this feeling in him still more deeply.

Melba advised him to drink more and have more frequent conjugal duties with her. He tried both of these, and actually became even more addicted to them, but his melancholy, far from disappearing, grew more pronounced and virulent.

He continued to lose weight, although his mental vigor, such as it was, remained unimpaired, and he spent all his time now recording his "conversations" with his former friends, who were still unable to see him owing to his marriage.

A few evenings before he died, he called Melba to his room and informed her that he had been bitten by a small buff-colored dog.

Melba greeted Malcolm vaguely, as she was nursing a hangover, and was still also a bit puzzled at having wakened up that morning to find herself in bed with Heliodoro, the Cuban valet, whose extreme handsomeness must have won her over to him in her cups.

Leaving the sickroom almost immediately, and a bit fed up being married to someone who would be sick, Melba decided on a longish drive with the Cuban as the best simple way of quieting her nerves, and it was already morning when she remembered Malcolm's remark about the dog bite.

To be on the safe side, she summoned a physician.

But it was, of course, as she remarked later to Heliodoro, just her luck, and a bit of a bit too late for medicine.

The physician, a man, who, as Melba noted immediately, looked fatally ill himself, gave this diagnosis: Malcolm was dying, he claimed, from acute alcoholism and sexual hyperaesthesia, and all that could be done for him now was give him every comfort and a quiet bed to himself.

Melba was going to tell the physician that nobody today died of the things he was accusing Malcolm of, but she felt there was no use having an argument if bereavement should come to the house.

"He is not dying, then, from a dog bite?" Melba inquired, taking the physician to the car which, she saw, was what must have at one time been a fairly decent Cadillac.

"There isn't a single bite on his body," the physician said, after a lengthy pause.

"He insists a dog bit him," Melba said, and she looked at her drink, which she had carried out with her to the car.

The physician, excusing his near forgetfulness, then hastily wrote out a prescription, which he handed to her.

Melba still waited on, her glass in hand, why she never under-

stood later, until the doctor got into his broken-down car and
drove off. She even waved to him from the drive with her glass.

Melba went into Malcolm's room and sat down quietly on the
bed by him.

When she looked into his face, she felt the physician might
be wrong in the diagnosis, but right about his taking a trip.

"Am I going to lose my little Number Three?" she inquired
softly so as not to disturb the boy too much.

Malcolm opened his eyes briefly and smiled.

"Do you know what is happening?" Melba asked.

"Call Madame Girard to come here," Malcolm said dryly. "I
can't remember all of my conversations with her, and can't get
it written down, you see. Mr. Cox, I know, wouldn't come,
because he is so happily married, or I might call him."

"You are going to die, kiddy," Melba said, taking his hand,
which bore her ring on it. She kissed the ring.

"Call Madame Girard and tell her to come," Malcolm
repeated.

"All right, kiddy. Can do," Melba said vaguely.

On being informed of Malcolm's grave condition, Madame
Girard left the the party which she was giving, and which she
had planned to last for three days, and drove to Melba's country
house.

Going in without announcing herself, Madame Girard
walked past Melba without so much as a greeting, and sat down
on the bed beside Malcolm.

Melba herself had taken a drug which would not allow her
to feel extreme grief or unpleasantness of any kind, and she was
content to leave Madame Girard and her husband together
while she went into the front room to practice her repertoire
for an evening performance.

Madame Girard wished, above all, to have Malcolm recognize her, not only because she now saw that it was Malcolm who
was the idea of her life—despite their short term of friendship
—but because she had so many things yet to tell him, including
Girard Girard's message of friendship to him, and his plea for

forgiveness for not having returned to the boy in the horticultural gardens last summer.

Madame Girard kept placing cold compresses on his forehead to relieve him of some of his fever.

As a reward for her patient care, there came a moment when he opened his eyes, and looked at her, but almost immediately closed them again.

A few minutes later, he said in his usual loud voice: "Estel Blanc on a white mare!"

Sometimes also he shouted "Hurrah!" but he never gave any evidence again that he had seen Madame Girard.

Several times during the evening, Madame Girard heard Melba singing her internationally famous number:

> I'm a little bit of this and that
> But I'm all one solid—

so that finally Madame Girard got up and closed the heavy inner door between the sickroom and Melba.

Madame Girard had come to stay, until everything was over.

Once, near the end, she thought that all of her patient waiting and care was indeed to be rewarded with "recognition," with a word to her from Malcolm, for the boy started up in bed, opened his eyes, and stared at her.

"Malcolm," she whispered.

"It's NOT twenty years!" he cried, and fell back again, without even seeing her.

Toward morning, Madame Girard heard Melba go out the front door, and a moment later the sound of the Daimler's motor.

Madame Girard had gone to the window to see if the Cuban valet was in the car with Melba, but in the dark she could not tell.

Returning to Malcolm's bed, she put her hand to his cheek.

"Prince!" she called out, feeling the iciness of his flesh.

She had missed, she saw immediately, his last single minute: Malcolm's short long life was at an end.

As Melba did not return that day, nor the next, nor did Madame Girard ever see her again, she herself took charge of the funeral ceremonies.

The florists of the town discussed Madame Girard's funeral expenditure for years to come. She had, for instance, ordered —even if she perhaps did not quite get—a quarter ton of roses, and an equal amount of violets, so that Malcolm's last hours above earth were passed in a greenhouse of sweetness and foliage.

One anonymous spray also arrived in what was perhaps meant to be the simulacrum of a bench.

Madame Girard, however, informed no one of the funeral. It was completely private so far as she was concerned and, so to speak, a command performance, with herself as the only audience.

She was greatly displeased, almost annihilated, however, that there was a ketchup factory in the vicinity, and since the ketchup season was at its peak at the time of Malcolm's funeral, the burned saccharine smell of tomatoes struggled desperately with the evanescent perfume of violets and roses.

Horses with black plumes in the European tradition carried the corpse to a small private burial ground purchased for the occasion by Madame Girard herself. A young military person who happened by chance to be in the neighborhood was asked to perform a trumpet voluntary, which he did creditably.

The only flaw in the ceremony was the repeated insistence of the local coroner and the undertaker—later they were both silenced, it is said, by money—that there had been no corpse at all, and that nobody was buried in the ceremony.

Thus, the only proof that Malcolm had died and was buried rested with Madame Girard herself, and in time her story became full of evasions.

But nobody could deny that there had been a ceremony, and that a casket had been lowered into a special plot, and that Madame Girard herself had been present at all of the aforementioned.

When the ceremony was over, Madame Girard saw, coming down the dusty country road on foot, none other than Girard Girard.

They exchanged looks, but did not speak, and then with a short glance at the freshly dug grave, Girard Girard accompanied his former wife back to an inn, where after a long silence, punctuated only by the sounds of their spoons moving in their coffee, Girard Girard excused himself and returned to the city.

Madame Girard, in any case, had long ago forgiven Girard Girard, since she never gave up her title or name, and continued to be the most effective individual force of her society.

She remained in the country until the following morning, looking over Malcolm's papers, and taking as many as she could find into her custody.

Since that day, Malcolm's grave, which has no marker beyond a stone bearing his name, has been poorly cared for and fallen into complete neglect, though since it was purchased in perpetuity, one can believe that his remains, if they are there, will be allowed to rest on for whatever portion of time may be reserved for the earth and the world.

A few years after the preceding events, Mr. Cox, through one of those rare second strokes of fortune, found another young man—a bit older, it is true than Malcolm—who became his pupil and went through over twenty-five addresses with the elder gentleman—and finally, much to Mr. Cox's surprise and even jealousy, took up an independent life-study of astrology, and entirely eclipsed his master.

Kermit, about two weeks after Malcolm's death, met a young, though retired, and very wealthy motion picture star, who was immediately taken with the little man, and they were married in a somewhat ostentatious ceremony in a suburb of San Francisco.

Eloisa Brace was awarded a life pension by an anonymous donor (who almost surely was Girard Girard) and was thus able to devote her entire waking life to painting, but her sudden security, many believed, destroyed her last vestiges of talent, and both she and her husband occupied themselves more and more with a program of social betterment for the community.

Estel Blanc became the successful entrepreneur of a small opera company, giving selections from the best modern operas, with Cora Naldi as permanent guest star.

Girard Girard, after a time, became the father of six male children—and this was for him the realization of a vague ambition and yearning which he had had, unconsciously, all along: the founding of a dynasty perpetuating his name.

Madame Girard was the constant companion of a young Italian biochemist, who shared the Château with her, and wished to marry her, but she refused to give up her "title," as she continued to call her name. The closeness of her association with the Italian, which became permanent, led (many believe) to her giving up the bottle entirely.

Melba was married in Yucatan to Heliodoro, the Cuban valet, with whom she had disappeared shortly before Malcolm's death. To everyone's surprise, she found herself reasonably contented and happy with him, remaining his wife for over five years. Her voice, however, has failed and she no longer sings publicly.

A year or so after Malcolm's supposed death, there was a somewhat convincing rumor that he was alive again, and the "favorite" of a circle much more advanced than the Cox-Girard-Brace consistory, but the rumor proved to be, finally, without foundation.

Everybody was surprised, nevertheless, after the talk about his being alive again had died down, to realize that Malcolm, in the interim, had been almost entirely forgotten, and was no longer a subject of conversation anywhere.

Madame Girard, however, though she never mentioned Malcolm—indeed she had no one to mention him to, since her new friends, such as the Italian biochemist, had never heard of him —Madame Girard continued to read with interest and surprise the three hundred pages of manuscript which Malcolm had left behind him, in French and English, his "conversations" with his friends, and although they had been written at times in delirium, and always in high fever, they continually held her attention, and she regretted he had not lived to record all the conversations he had ever had with all whom he had ever met.

Thomas McGuane

NINETY-TWO IN THE SHADE

A refugee from a world of drug addicts and misfits, Thomas Skelton goes home to Key West, Florida, but Key West itself turns out to be an alien world—torrid, hostile, grotesque. Taking up residence in an abandoned airplane fuselage, Skelton plans to become a skiff guide in the shining blue subtropical waters—even though another guide, resenting competition, now promises to kill him. . . . "Like Mailer and Pynchon, Thomas McGuane makes the page, the paragraph, the sentence itself a record of continuous imaginative activity. . . . He is an important as well as brilliant novelist"—*The New York Times Book Review.*

Ernest Hebert

THE DOGS OF MARCH

In the New Hampshire hills, tame dogs turn savage at the start of spring, pursuing winter-weakened deer through thinning snows. It is a senseless and cruel pursuit—the awakening of some primitive instinct in dogs supposed to be domesticated. Howard Elman also feels pursued —he's unemployed, his wife suffers from hysterical paralysis, his son rejects him, and his rich new neighbor is plotting to take over his land —and so in Howard, as in the dogs of March, there is a sudden surge of violence. . . . "What makes *The Dogs of March* a brilliant book is Mr. Hebert's ability to portray ordinary people. . . . He catches them so exactly that one feels a rush of love and recognition, of common humanity"—*The New York Times.*

Maureen Howard

BEFORE MY TIME

Laura Quinn, forty years old, a successful Boston journalist and the mother of two, is established from the outset of this witty, insightful novel as a woman settled in her situation. When a rebellious eighteen-year-old relative, Jim Cogan, comes to her Cambridge household from the diametrically opposed world of the Bronx, Laura's universe is profoundly shaken. Maureen Howard's precise, exactingly crafted prose carries this story of a woman's growing self-knowledge, of familial ties and conflicts, and of generational differences into the realm of revelation.

H. E. Bates

LOVE FOR LYDIA

Lydia is a beautiful English girl growing up in the 1920s. She is also wayward, passionate, utterly unpredictable. "Don't ever stop loving me . . . even if I'm bad to you," she demands of her lover, Richardson, and Richardson swears that he will never stop. How can he know that love for Lydia will be so dangerous? . . . *Love for Lydia* has been a recently acclaimed TV dramatic series. "A compelling story . . . vital in its characterizations, and especially rich in its rendering of natural and seasonal detail"—*The New York Times Book Review*.

Robertson Davies

FIFTH BUSINESS

Fifth Business, which one critic said was "as masterfully executed as anything in the history of the novel," might be described simply as the life of a Canadian schoolteacher named Dunstan Ramsay. Such a description, however, would not even suggest the dark currents of love, ambition, vengeance, and death that flow through this powerful work, cast in the form of Ramsay's memoirs. As Ramsay writes, he reveals his influence on other people: on Percy Staunton, who, one day in 1908, threw a snowball with a stone in it; on Mary Dempster, whom it hit; on Paul Dempster, her son, born prematurely because of the blow; and on the ravishingly beautiful Leola Cruikshank, whom Staunton grew up to marry and, eventually, to destroy. *Fifth Business* is the first novel in the celebrated "Deptford trilogy" that also includes *The Manticore* and *World of Wonders,* each one of which can stand alone as a novel of passion, intelligence, and suspense.

THE MANTICORE

A manticore is a monster with the head of a man, the body of a lion, and the tail of a scorpion. . . . The Canadian David Staunton enters Jungian analysis in Switzerland because of his father's strange death. (Was it an accident? Or suicide? Or homicide?) As the analysis proceeds, the manticore is among the symbols that emerge, and David learns surprising things not only about himself but also about his father, Percy, about the schoolmaster Dunstan Ramsay, about the libidinous Liesl Naegeli, and about the warped and gifted Magnus Eisengrim.

WORLD OF WONDERS

Magnus Eisengrim is a master illusionist, and together with his friends Dunstan Ramsay and Liesl Naegeli, he is ensconced at Liesl's castle in Switzerland, where he is acting the title role in a film. The film's great Scandinavian director, Jurgen Lind, draws from him an account of his life story, a story as rich in color, drama, comedy, and gripping tension as any in recent fiction.

Graham Greene

THE END OF THE AFFAIR

This frank, intense account of a love affair and its mystical aftermath takes place in a suburb of wartime London.

THE POWER AND THE GLORY

In one of the southern states of Mexico, during an anticlerical purge, the last priest, like a hunted hare, is on the run. Too human for heroism, too humble for martyrdom, the little worldly "whiskey priest" is nevertheless impelled toward his squalid Calvary as much by his own efforts as by the efforts of his pursuers.

THE QUIET AMERICAN

The Quiet American is a terrifying portrait of innocence at large, a wry comment on European interference in Asia in its story of the Franco-Vietminh war in Vietnam. While the French Army is grappling with the Vietminh, back at Saigon a young, high-minded American begins to channel economic aid to a "Third Force." The narrator, a seasoned foreign correspondent, is forced to observe: "I never knew a man who had better motives for all the trouble he caused."

Also:
BRIGHTON ROCK
A BURNT-OUT CASE
THE COMEDIANS
THE HEART OF THE MATTER
IT'S A BATTLEFIELD
JOURNEY WITHOUT MAPS
LOSER TAKES ALL
MAY WE BORROW YOUR HUSBAND?
THE MINISTRY OF FEAR
OUR MAN IN HAVANA
THE PORTABLE GRAHAM GREENE
SHADES OF GREENE
TRAVELS WITH MY AUNT

William S. Burroughs

EXTERMINATOR!

Conspirators plot to explode a train carrying nerve gas. . . . Intending to pacify the world, a scientist miscalculates and releases a fatal virus. . . . Patients activate a death ray to destroy the doctors, nurses, and "vile cooks" in a hospital. . . . A perfect servant suddenly reveals himself to be the insidious Dr. Fu Manchu. . . . Science-fantasy, war, racism, corporation capitalism, drug addiction, and various medical and psychiatric horrors play their parts in this dazzling, mosaiclike novel about exterminators of all kinds, from the individual ("Personally I prefer a pyrethrum job to a fluoride") to the cosmic and collective. Said the London *Times Literary Supplement:* "Nobody manages to make so much sense of insane violence as Burroughs does by reducing it to spectacle, a drug of unreality without which Western civilization—which mistakes its own materialism for realism—cannot get by."

JUNKY

Here is the first complete and unexpurgated edition of one of the most powerful books ever written about drug addiction. Following its hero from his Midwestern birthplace to New York City, New Orleans, and Mexico City, *Junky* depicts the addict's life—his hallucinations, his ghostly nocturnal wanderings, his strange sexuality, his hunger for the needle. Above all, these searing pages present a shocking demonstration of the junk equation: "Junk is not, like alcohol or weed, a means to increased enjoyment of life. Junk is not a kick. It is a way of life."

Jack Kerouac

ON THE ROAD

This is the novel that put Jack Kerouac and the beat generation on the national map and the best-seller lists. Concerned with a group of exuberantly uninhibited young Americans, the narrative roars back and forth across the continent and down to Mexico in one of the most fantastic journeys ever to appear in American literature. The book is ultimately a celebration of life itself, a lyrical yea-saying outburst from one of the few truly original talents to career down the literary pike in many a year. "A historic occasion . . . the most beautifully executed, the clearest, and the most important utterance yet made by the generation Kerouac himself named years ago as 'beat,' and whose principal avatar he is"—Gilbert Millstein, *The New York Times*.

THE DHARMA BUMS

This novel appeared just a year after the author's explosive *On the Road*. The same expansiveness, humor, and contagious zest for life that sparked the earlier novel spark this one but through a more cohesive story. The principals are two ebullient young men engaged in a passionate search for dharma, or truth. Their major adventure is the pursuit of the Zen way, which takes them climbing into the High Sierras to seek the lesson of solitude—a lesson that has a hard time surviving their forays into the pagan groves of San Francisco's Bohemia, with its marathon wine-drinking bouts, poetry jam sessions, experiments in "yabyum," and similar nonascetic pastimes.

James Salter

SOLO FACES

Solo Faces is a novel as extraordinary as its subject—men who climb mountains. The men are Vernon Rand and Jack Cabot, locked in a fierce rivalry forged in a deep friendship. Above all, it is the story of Rand and the purity with which he gives himself to the mountains, and the subtle but sure revelation of the loss of that purity as the story follows him from the rock faces of California to the icy majesty of the Alps. *Solo Faces* tells of bravery and death, trust and betrayal, and, finally, a peace fought for and won.

Edmund White

NOCTURNES FOR THE KING OF NAPLES

This hauntingly beautiful novel is an evocation of a lost love—a love evoked through a ghostly sequence of nocturnal visions . . . of New York, Spain, Greece, and other places whose exact locations are not revealed. Following a strange, elegant, and musical order of dream-images, these "nocturnes" recreate the longings of childhood, the regrets of the pleasure-seeker, the bitterness of desertion, the ambiguities of homosexual love.